GRIM
FUTURE

VOLUME 2

DAVID KONKOL

ISBN number: 978-1-7359785-3-6

Written by David Konkol
Instagram madoverlordstudios

Webpage www.madoverlordstudios.com
Cover Art: Chris Puglise https://cpuglise9.artstation.com/

Interior Map: Dan Smith

INTRODUCTION

This whole book is an experiment.

In the first volume of the Grim Future stories, I presented them as: one story in the 'modern age', albeit with some cybernetics, genetics, and superheroes, the next story showing the repercussions of what had happened in the story before it to the age that the Covered Man resides in. The story following would be part of the Covered Man time-line but would have little to do with the previous stories. It had a very 'comic book without the comic art' feel to it.

This volume expands on that idea.

To follow the logical progression of comics, there would be long story arcs through multiple types of comics (Batman would be film noir, Spider-man was a teenage drama, while Punisher bordered on war comics and so on). So, you'd have these huge, sometimes year long story lines that would have to 'adjust' to different types of comics.

That is what I am attempting here.

Some stories are horror, some adventure, a cyberpunk noir mystery, but the tale of the ruins of Black Earth Wisconsin and what happens to it, is at the heart of the book (okay, the first story is more of a bridge between volume one and volume two, but there is a stone tower in Whitewater WI that is perfect for an homage to one of my favorite Robert E. Howard tales, 'The Black Stone"

Hope you enjoy reading this as much as I had writing it.

CONTENTS

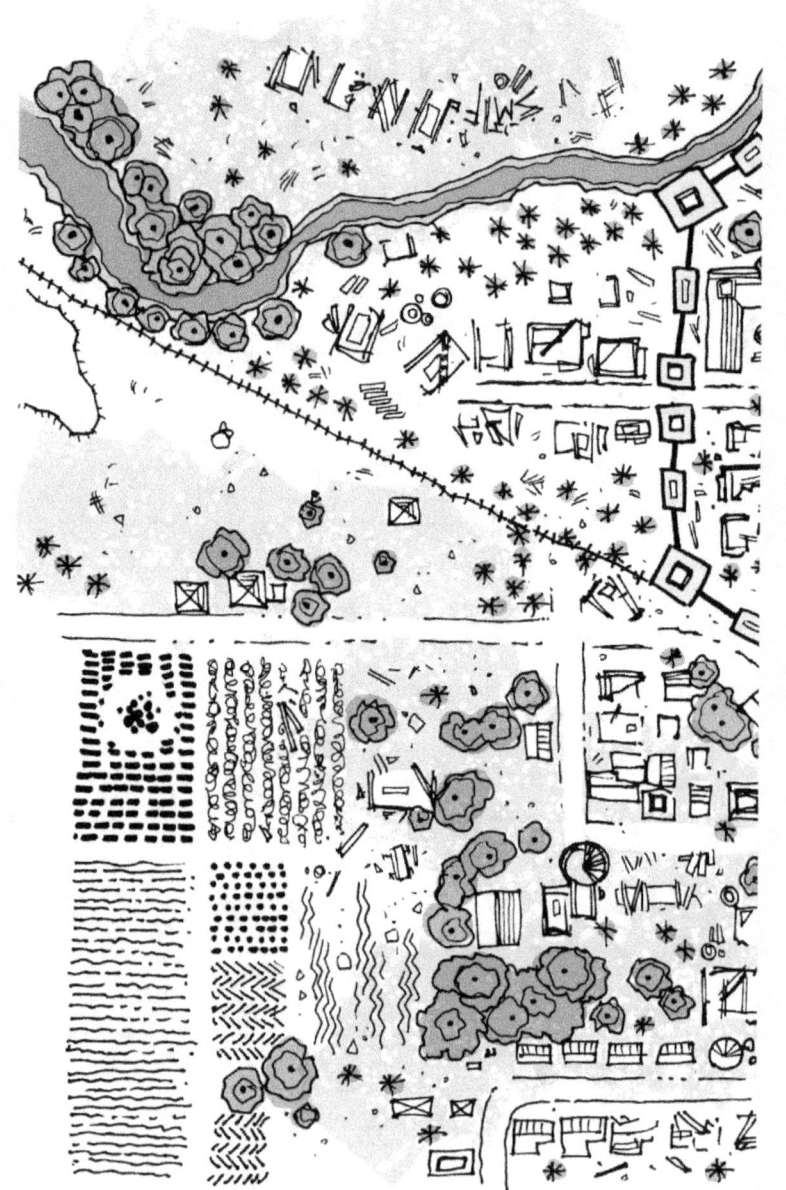

STORY ONE

The Stone Tower of Watertown

The black car raced along the remnants of Highway 59, now just called 'the 59', along the edge of the Shallow Sea. Once fertile farmland, the cracked moon shifted the tides, putting an ocean where there wasn't any before.

"Ocean" might not be the right word. Rumor had it, one could walk quite far out into the Shallow Sea without your head even getting wet. Few tried this however, for things lurked in those waters. Things that could devour one whole.

Swerving around a broken chunk of broken road, the black car almost slammed into a rusty derelict truck. Only the quick reflexes of the driver turned the collision into a near miss. The driver was a huge brute of a man, covered head to toe in a black suit, except for the round goggles that covered his eyes.

As he continued speeding down the highway, he grumbled to himself. He was driving northeast, and he wanted to be going northwest, but the Jane Gang blocked 'the 90.' Suddenly, dozens of thuggos erupted from hidey-holes alongside the road. He only had a few bullets and shells left, so he pushed the gas pedal to the floor and fled up 'the 59', away from his intended destination.

The road began to narrow. A settlement appeared on the horizon. The ruined and collapsed buildings were huddled together as if for protection from a ruined, uncaring world. He slowed to maneuver around several abandoned cars at an old intersection. The road he crossed wandered out into the Shallow Sea on his right. To the left, it just ended, the asphalt gone.

Trees had started to push themselves up out of the ground where the road used to be. All gnarled and bent, they ranged from saplings to young trees. They grew leaves, but they didn't have the green lush foliage of the BeforeTimes; these were grayish and wilted. Each leaf grasping onto the branch as a drowning man grasps a floating piece of driftwood.

He continued onward.

As the highway ended and became a smaller street, he found what he was looking for, the junction to 'the N.' The Covered Man silently cursed under the material of his suit.

The entire way was blocked with abandoned vehicles. Some even piled two cars high. Along either side of the road were sharp stakes pounded into the ground for at least a hundred meters, maybe more. Someone didn't want anyone traveling down 'the N,' he thought.

He had the strength to clear all of this wreckage away, but it would take hours. Not to mention the noise would surely alert anyone nearby, a perfect opportunity for the nameless denizens of what remained of civilization to sneak up on him.

He glanced at the setting sun. It would be dark in about an hour. Leaving himself exposed at night was a death wish.

He had to refuel. The tank still remained two-thirds full, but more than once, making sure the tank stayed full allowed him to flee pursuers, saving his life.

After he got out of the car, he strode to the back, glancing sideways for signs of danger while the goggles made it look like he constantly looked forward. He reached into the trunk and grabbed the empty Jerry can stowed there. Tapping the fuel storage drum, he determined the drum was less than a third of the way full. He would have to scrounge for fuel soon.

He surveyed the skeletal remains of the area as the Jerry can filled. A way off to the north, he spotted a thick forest of the same twisted trees. Above those contorted branches, a stone tower could be seen.

After filling the tank, he pulled a rag from his belt and wiped off the nozzle, then replaced it. Slamming the trunk closed, he reached into one of his belt pouches and pulled out a map so ancient its age could be pegged from the fact it was printed on paper.

Unfolding the map, he studied it. He noticiced the shadows getting long. He flicked a button on his goggles for night vision, but he recalled the charge ran out weeks ago. With a sigh, he removed a flashlight from his belt and made a mental note to search for batteries.

He found himself in Water Town. 'The N' would have taken him almost directly west, between The Jane and Mad Town. As dangerous as The Jane was, he would rather drive through blindfolded than brave the outskirts of Mad Town.

Folding the map, he replaced it in his belt. He took a step to walk around to the driver's seat when he saw a shadowy human form run between two sections of broken wall on the other side of the street.

Instantly, the sawed-off was in his hand.

"Saw you."

The only reply was a gentle breeze that from the trees, blowing the lighter garbage in a circular dance across the abandoned street.

The Covered Man did not want to get back in his vehicle yet, since whoever was there would have a perfect chance to ambush him while he started the car. He took a few steps closer to the ruined section of wall, the rustling garbage making more noise than his footsteps.

Reaching the edge of the wall, he snapped around the corner, brandishing his weapon in front of him.

Nothing was there.

The section of the wall was about two meters tall and about three meters long. Nothing else was near but another section of the same. Nothing lay behind that section either. He glanced from one broken area to the other to ensure he didn't miss a detail in the early evening gloom.

Then he heard his car startup. By the time he spun around, the car had squealed its tires and took off to the north. His legs pushed him in the direction of the vehicle speeding away. He stretched his arm toward it, not even close to grabbing the vehicle. His muscles propelling him harder than any "normal" human could, but he still couldn't catch his car.

Watching as his car drove up the street. He lost sight of the vehicle and the tower, both blocked by the thick overgrown forest. Racing onward, he heard the engine of his car sputter and stop.

The road opened into a small clearing around the base of the tower. The car was there, engine off, and the driver's door wide open. The Covered Man stopped to catch his breath, pointing his weapon at every lengthening shadow he could see.

After a few moments, he realized he was the only thing moving in the area, he lowered his weapon but did not holster it. Stepping up to the car, he peered in the windows, checking to see if everything was still there. When it appeared everything was still in place, he scanned the area again for any sign of the thief.

Looking up, he noticed the foreboding tower above him. The structure was built with stone and looked ancient. He saw the ruins of a short wall that surrounded the taller structure. Now knocked to the ground, only its foundation remaining.

The tower had freshly bored holes in the mortar, all shoulder height. What the holes were used for, there was no clue.

Seeing no sign of whoever drove the car here, the Covered Man decided not to spend the night but instead take his chances finding a section of street that could lead him out of town. Even if it meant he had to drive back the way he came. He had strode to the open driver-side door, finally holstered his weapon, and started to get in when he heard a scream.

To the west, at the edge of the forest, were a few crumbling buildings about four stories tall. Atop of the building made of tan brick, he could see some humanoid figures. He couldn't make them out, but one of the figures was the source of the outcries.

Shutting the car door, he crouched low and moved from tree trunk to tree trunk, trying to get a closer view of the source of the screams. It wouldn't be the first time raiders used screaming people to get the naive a reason to rush in, only to be ambushed.

He crossed a section of ground that used to be a road or a parking lot. The grass and trees pushed up from the earth. Only an occasional chunk of asphalt gave a hint to what originally was here.

Reaching the edge of the wood line, he could see a few figures on top of the building. They were human. It looked like about two dozen of them, all hung on wooden poles by chains around their hands. Even at this distance, he could see that some had been dead for at least a month or more. The crows that lurked on the nearby stone outcroppings of the building avoided them.

Those that screamed appeared to have been chained there only in the past few days. No visible signs of starvation were evident. No sign of their captors were nearby. Thinking, he decided began to resume his plan to get in his car and leave, but the screams pierced the thin veil to his past. He told himself that any humans he saved would owe him. People owing you favors are the only currency that mattered in this world of decay. The Covered Man formulated a plan to free those still alive and make it back to his car before he was discovered.

He leaped to the second-story window, and using the sills and the ledges of the building, he shimmied up its side. Throwing one of his powerful arms over the lip of the top floor, he pulled himself all the way to the roof.

The roof was empty.

The Covered Man looked behind every stone outcropping and every structure. He was certain he saw people chained up here. But there was no sign of them now.

Scanning the surface for any sign of blood, he found nothing save for a few indentations where wooden poles might have been. It looked as if no one had touched them for weeks. Kneeling to inspect these indentations closer, he did find a few tufts of hair and skin; the edges of the drying flesh crumbled as he picked them up to examine them. They were all similar in size, as if someone dug fingernails or claws deep into their victims.

Evening had fully set in at this point. The Covered Man wanted to make one more quick search of the entire roof, just to make sure he wasn't crazy, and then get out of there. The bodily remains he found were a few weeks old, but something odd was happening. He now just wanted to put as much road between him and this place as fast as possible, survivors or not.

As the Covered Man finished his last round, he still had no new information, not even more new remains of whomever was torn apart on that abandoned rooftop.

He approached the lip of the building and prepared to make his way back to his car. As he swung his leg over the edge to begin his descent, the ground around the structure adjacent to the one he stood upon lit up, as great campfires sparked into life. Screams and screeches broke the silence of the infant evening. These weren't screams of humans in pain or even seeking help. They were inhuman voices, crying out in anticipation of the evening's hunt.

The fiendish gibbering rose up over the buildings, and the Covered Man felt certain that whatever he saw, or thought he saw had something to do with these monsters.

It was not his problem.

"Only fools face off against unknown numbers of enemies for no reward," he thought. He would sneak back down to his vehicle and make his escape before those twisted crawlers of a world long forgotten, even knew he was there.

The broken moon gave off little light, but it was enough to assist him as he scaled down the side of the building. Once he reached the ground, he slipped back into the protection of the tall grass, heading in the direction of the tower and his car.

Moving like a whisper through the tall grass and weeds, other sounds of the evening began to arise as he left the ruined structures behind him. The chirping of crickets and the hoots of owls, with the death cry of some small animal when a nameless predator caught it could be heard.

His car and the tower next to it emerged from the encroaching darkness of the forest. With only a sliver of the fading sunset remaining, he would be at a distinct disadvantage at night until he recharged his goggles.

Emerging from the tall grass, he made his way to the side of his vehicle. As he grasped the handle to open the door, he felt the presence of someone being nearby. Looking back over his shoulder, he could see three mutants standing directly behind him. One looked like a lizard, another - a hawk, and the last like a gorilla with several human baby legs sticking out of it at odd angles. The gorilla mutant wielded a section of rebar in its twisted hands. Dozens of other mutants crept out of the darkness.

Before the Covered Man could move, the gorilla-like mutant growled, "Smelt the gas, human."

The mutant brought down the section of rebar onto the back of his head, and the world went black.

><<<

The world spun as the Covered Man regained consciousness. He could feel restraints around his wrist that held him upright. His head ached so bad he could barely lift it to look around. Gazing at his feet, he could see that he had been chained to the base of the tower.

"You took quite a blow for a human… If you are a human under all that." The hawk-looking mutant from earlier spoke to him.

With all of his might, the Covered Man lifted his head. Dozens of mutants stood around him. They had a huge bonfire going about ten paces away. He could feel the searing heat, even through the protective nature of his suit.

The hawk spoke to him again, "Figure you must have some kind of disease, wearing that suit. That makes you not good for eat, but you serve in other ways." The hawk nodded at the rest of the mutants, as some sort of signal, who began to hum or emit a low growl depending on if they had lips or not. The voices soon combined into a rhythmic chant.

The Covered Man tried to lunge forward to attack his captor but couldn't. Several dozen chains held him tight, held in place by a few eye screws, pounded into the mortar between the stone blocks of the tower.

"Given enough time you might be able to break those chains. But you won't have the chance." The hawk mutant looked up the side of the tower and then backed up a few steps. "Thank you for your vehicle," It said, pointing a taloned claw at the black car on the edge of the light of the blazing fire, "Once we learn its secrets, it will allow us to expand our reach," it then held up the Covered Man's sawed-off, "And for your weapons. They will assist us as we raid the surrounding settlements for food and slaves."

The Covered Man said, "Humans on the roof?"

The hawk mutant looked confused and looked from the Covered Man to the roof and back. We hung the food up there when we first captured the settlement. "But there hasn't been humans on that roof for weeks, maybe months." The hawk looked at the other nearby mutants in disbelief. "Another insane human. Such a fragile species," he said with a jagged edge of contempt.

The gorilla mutant replied, "Are there any other kind?" They both chuckled at the joke. The laugh was terrifying.

The Covered Man lunged forward again, breaking a few of the chains. This startled the hawk mutant, but instead of moving forward to restrain him, it joined in the chanting. Gazing up the side of the tower again, this time with fear flashing across its inhuman features. It motioned with its feathered, talon-like hand for the rest of the mutants to chant faster.

It was the gorilla who stepped forward and again brought the section of rebar down upon the Covered Man's head, making his body go limp again. It did not step backward like the hawk, but instead held the rebar on its shoulder, ready to strike again if need be.

The chanting grew louder. Wings, talons, and clawed hands all reached skyward in unison. The Covered Man tried to raise his head again, this time to see what the mutants were grasping at.

At the top of the tower, thick fog had formed and began to swirl about like a maelstrom. As the fog picked up speed, a faint eye could be seen forming in its center, directly above the tower. As the eye appeared, tendrils of fog began to creep down the side of the tower. The gorilla mutant stepped back with caution and laughed its ghastly alien laugh.

The Covered Man strained his muscles to tear out a section of chain and free his arm. Whip-like, he lashed it around the hawk mutant's neck, and jerking it hard, pulled the hawk mutant off balance. The gorilla mutant stepped forward again, rebar raised.

The Covered Man's foot snapped out, catching the gorilla right in the groin, sending it tumbling to the ground, letting go of the rebar it held. The mutants howled in panic and anger as they realized what was happening.

The Covered Man snatched the section of rebar out of the air and inserted it into a link of the chain and twisted as hard as he could, snapping it clean.

He put his foot against the wall of the tower and pushed with all his might, straining the rest of the chains. Another mutant stepped forward and got smashed across the head for its troubles.

The chains snapped, freeing the Covered Man. The mutants screamed in terror, but they were not looking at him; they watched as the feelers of fog grabbed the hawk mutant and dragged it up into the air.

Four of the mutants grabbed at the hawk mutant, trying to pull it back to earth. They were rewarded by being ensnared by other tendrils, like insects stuck on the leaf of a sundew plant. Other mutants stood rooted to the ground, afraid of the maelstrom at the top of the tower they had help summon. An otherworldly thing that now grasped five of their kind and dragging them upward.

The hawk headed mutant struck the swirls of clouds near the forming eye. The mutant's scream echoed off the nearby hills as he sunk into the cloud upward until he dissolved away. The white of the eye flushed red and the pupil rolled to the side in a gesture of euphoria.

While everyone's attention was staring upward at what they unleashed, the Covered Man took advantage of the situation, pulling his chains the rest of the way out of the tower.

The pain of the gorilla mutant began to reside, glanced at the thing devouring its comrades above it and spotted its prey escaping.

"The Human! The Human!" it shouted as it moved to intercept its prey amidst the chaos. With a furry muscled arm, it slammed its fist into the Covered Man's chin, sending him tumbling backwards into the tower.

The gorilla mutant grabbed the Covered Man's head between his powerful arms. Smoky tendrils crept down the side of the stone structure from another age. Like a chameleon's tongue, a tendril struck the dog faced mutant, jerking it upward. It struck the swirling smoke like hitting concrete, then got enveloped into the bizarre swirling vapor like sinking into a downy pillow, its edges dissolving away the further it sunk in.

The Covered Man slammed his free hand against the mutant gorilla's powerful arms but to no avail. He saw one of the smoky tendrils creep across the stone surface of the tower, now about three feet from his head.

"I'll feed you to that thing, you relic of the past!" its powerful arms crushing the air from even the Covered Man's lungs. Striking the gorilla mutant with his free hand, and still not making it budge.

The other hand smashed the rebar across the gorilla's nose, again and again; blood trickled from its nose.

"You are not match for me human! There hasn't been a furless one yet that could break my grip!"

The smoky tendril struck, wrapping around the Covered Man's free arm. The gorilla mutant let go of him so he could be dragged off to his fate, only to have the Covered Man jam the section of rebar into its neck, through its head and piercing the top of its skull.

The Covered Man felt himself being hoisted into the air. Releasing the rebar, he instead grabbed the gorilla mutant by the head and pushed the dying mutant against the wispy thing that held him.

Blood from the wound in its neck washed over the ghastly appendage. The thing quickly let go of the Covered Man and drove its wispy tendril into the gorilla mutant's neck and began to hoist it upward. The red of the alien eye turned darker.

Landing on the ground, the Covered Man sprinted toward his car, slamming his shoulder into a lizard-like mutant, sending it sprawling.

As the Covered Man got into the black car, the engine roared to life. The rest of the mutants trembled in fear as the gorilla mutant managed a gurgling scream as it disappeared into the maelstrom. Watching what happened to the strongest among them, the remaining mutants turned and ran.

Speeding away, he struck a few of the mutants, crushing them under wheel or sending them sprawling into the thick trees and grass. Turning toward the old campus, he roared through it to reach the road he saw from the roof earlier.

13

The Covered Man swerved through the brick structures, and dipped into a small ditch to have his car hit the road on the other side of it. Tires squealed as he turned the wheel hard to straighten his vehicle to flee northward. He cursed the loss of his weapons, and his jerry can. Peeking through the trees as he drove, the maelstrom had disappeared and only the lone top of the stone tower remained.

STORY TWO

The Rise of Blac Arth

The Covered Man got out of the black car to look at the ruined town. Many of the buildings were in a state of disrepair, and most of the sick-looking trees had lost their leaves, even though summer just began.

The figure had a black body suit from head to toe, with only leather boots, gloves, belt and metallic goggles to break the space.

He swore he heard a metal grinder from a machine shop as he drove up. Now, all he heard was the creaking of nearby trees in a slight breeze. On the north side of the street was an abandoned gas station. The pumps were gone, and not a shard of glass remained in the panes in the building. Farther west, there used to be some kind of structure, but now it lay in ruins.

On the south side of 'the 14', stood a one-story building. A man in green overalls leaned against the side of it, his hands in his pockets, watching him. Directly in front of the man was an old-style garbage can. On the dead grass between the structure and the road was a sign, three feet high and six feet long, with yellow letters on a black background that read, "Welc me to Blac Arth."

The Covered Man walked toward the building. After taking a few steps, the man in green overalls shouted to him, "Just keep your hands away from your weapons and there won't be any trouble."

Instinctively, the Covered Man scanned the rooftops of nearby buildings for snipers.

"We aren't fixin' to shoot ya unless you cause trouble. And despite your strange get-up, you don't look like the trouble startin' type. You look like the tradin' type. Am I right?"

"Yeah."

"Well, then welcome to the settlement of Blac Arth, stranger. Where'd you get the fancy duds?"

"Got car scrap?"

A voice from the trash can said, "This guy speaks less than Joshua." The lid opened and a young girl of about fifteen or sixteen popped out. Her skin was sickly and pale. It looked like she hadn't eaten real food in weeks. Her light brown hair lay matted to her head, sticky with filth. She had a rust coated pistol in her hand.

The man smiled at the girl as she tucked the gun in her holster, which was made for both a person much larger than her and the pistol she carried. "Sure sounds that way," he said, "but we are always willing to trade with decent folk. Even if they are dressed like a garbage bag with goggles." Detaching himself from the wall he leaned on and running his fingers through his shaggy graying beard, he asked, "Got a name?"

"Yeah."

After a moment's silence, the man said, "You're a charmer, aren't you?" He glanced at the girl, who was dusting herself off. He then looked back at the stranger and said, "Well, Trash Bag, my name's Rays. That there is my pride and joy, Kristine." Kristine looked at her father and smiled.

Rays turned and walked around the corner of the building toward a larger structure at the end of the street, directly behind the one they had been standing in front of.

"The wife's in the store, what we call The Box," He nodded toward the dwelling he had been leaning against. "But we aren't going in yet. We have to see Joshua in The Shop. While the wifey takes care of selling supplies, we keep most of the heavy-duty vehicle stuff in The Shop." He nodded at the metal building they strode towards.

It was a story and a half tall and made of metal. Two large garage doors were set in the side facing the road, and a normal sized door lie between them. The left hand garage door was open and the white-hot flame flared from someone welding inside, lighting the space even from fifty yards away.

Kristine and the Covered Man followed Rays. She made sure she always stayed a little to the side and about a step behind him, eyes locked on the knife and the holsters that hung from his belt.

She eyed the empty holster. "You're missing a gun?"

"Yeah."

"Did you lose it, or was it taken from you?"

The Covered Man remained silent as he kept walking.

"Bet you lost it. Left it behind somewhere, I gather."

Reaching the dragon's-maw-like door of the building, the Covered Man said to Rays, "Just you four?"

"Two others," Rays said. "David lives here as well. In that building on the other side of Canal Street." He pointed to a small one-floor cottage that lay across the road from The Box, engulfed by vines and weeds. "Nice enough guy. Not as handy as Joshua and I, but man, he can play a fiddle like you wouldn't believe."

Rays smiled at a memory of music and happiness. When he gazed over at the unmoving, blank stare of the Covered Man's goggles, his dream turned into an unnerved cough, and he continued. "The other settler is Manny." Rays went quiet for a moment. "Once, he ran with local raiders, but he settled here with us. One of the best rifle shots I know. He's probably out hunting.

"We have quite a few outliers that come in to trade from time to time. No one wants to stay, since any large group of people these days attracts unwanted attention."

With one hand, he shielded his eyes from the welding torch. With the other, he pounded on the metal wall. "Hey Joshua! We got a trader here!"

The flame dimmed and the man inside removed his welding mask. He put a cigarette in his mouth and lit it with the welding torch, then shut it off and laid it on the bench.

Joshua came out and squinted as he passed the threshold from the dark interior. His sandy brown hair was shaggy and unkempt. He wore red overalls and sneakers, both dirty from working in the garage. A belt hung around his waist with a pistol attached.

Blowing a cloud of smoke from the side of his mouth, he looked the newcomer over and said, "Yeah?"

Kristine grinned at the man's curt reply.

The Covered Man said, "Need parts for the car."

"Wheel it in and we will see what we can do. What are you trading?"

"Food. Bullets. Various weapons."

Joshua's hand went to his pistol. "You a raider?"

"No. It's *donated*."

Joshua glanced down to the weapons on the Covered Man's belt, then back to his black, expressionless goggles. "I'm sure we have parts for you somewhere."

Joshua walked over to one of the metal racks inside the shed and dug through the crude cardboard boxes lining them.

Rays grinned back at his daughter and said, "I think I said more today than these two said all year combined."

Kristine giggled in reply.

If the Covered Man heard either of them, he made no indication. Instead, he looked at the six cots in the corner of the large metal building. They were dirty and stained, and seemed to be on their last legs. In the opposite corner was a makeshift fire pit with a metal tube leading to the ceiling for exhaust. Several cracked plates were set on a carved wooden bench nearby, with only rocks and sticks as primitive utensils.

"Everyone lives here?"

Rays nodded. "Yup. Welcome to The Shop." He stretched out his arms to formally present the structure. "The most defensible building in town. Speaking of, we can throw in a hot meal if you help us move our stuff from The Box back here. We move the stuff to the Box during the day to trade, but evening's comin'. Raiders and worse will be prowlin' about, and we need to get our all that gear back where it will be safe."

Joshua ashed his cigarette, "Pull your ride into here, so I can work on it."

The Covered Man left and soon returned with the black car, slowly pulling it into The Shop so it could be worked on.

Rays beckoned the Stranger to follow him to The Box, "Joshua will take good care of it while we get the stuff. Trade is life these days, and folks won't survive long as a trading outpost if they rob people. You should be more worried about what prowls this area at night. Raiders. And worse.

><u>w</u><

Evening was just creeping up as the Covered Man carried the last of the trading supplies from The Box into The Shop. Screams and cries of things both human and inhuman echoed through the ruins just a few blocks away to the south. Joshua closed the large door and locked it tight, then checked the smaller door to make sure it was locked as well.

Rays and his wife, Linda, were busy cooking over the fire pit. Her dark skin and deep brown eyes sparkled every time she looked at Rays. His eyes reflecting the sentiment back to her.

From the smell, the Covered Man wasn't sure if they were burning something on purpose or were horrible cooks.

There were two others that the Covered Man had not met, sitting around the cooking fire with them. An older, grizzled man with a bushy hair and beard, both almost completely gray, dressed in a faded red shirt and denim overalls. A fiddle case sat on the floor next to his chair, marking him as David.

The man next to him had a stiff leather jacket, heavily cracked from age. He also had a beard, but his was trimmed neatly. His hair was groomed in a similar fashion, and also frosted. Traces of the original black color still lingered in his eyebrows and roots. The rifle slung over his shoulder marked him as Manny the huntsman.

They all found something to sit on and huddled near the fire, awaiting their meager meal.

Something slammed into the locked doors and gibbered and babbled as it repeatedly threw itself at the metal barriers, searched for a way to open them. The Covered Man tensed, but the others did not seem panicked or upset by the clamor. But there was something there. Even the jovial Rays had a dour look on his face, likely knowing those doors would only hold so long. Someday, whatever was outside would break in. Yet, they seemed to accept it, as though what lie outside was inevitable.

Linda took a scoop of whatever was in the pot and put it on a cracked plate, then a second scoop. As she dished out the second plate, Rays placed a carved stone spoon on the side of the plate and handed it to the Covered Man.

The others got their portion of the meager stew as the Covered Man picked up the stone tool and stirred his. Water, some kind of meat, and wilted cabbage or spinach were all it contained.

As if he knew what the Covered Man was thinking, Manny said, "Tough hunting today. Only saw one rabbit that looked safe to eat." He broke eye contact and stared at the floor.

The Covered Man was about to try the meal when something beat against the small, side door. It bent in a bit before returning to its normal shape. Manic babbling and human-like howls came from outside. He waited for a reaction from the others.

"The rest of the *settlers*," David said in a sarcastic tone, nodding at the door. "When things fell apart, hey fled Mad Town. Came out here and… Well, became what they became. As the world around them crumbled, they withdrew into whatever basic primitive desires they could to alleviate the pain of living. As a result, their minds cracked and their primal instincts took over."

Linda interrupted, "As they fed their lizard brain, they became their lizard brain."

Manny nodded and added, "And this is even before Fappa Jack and his raiders came."

The Covered Man leaned forward. "You remember what happened?"

David stroked his beard, "Sure do. It was the glory days of humanity."

The Covered Man asked, "How did the Collapse actually happen?" His hand drifted to the pistol on his belt.

David moved his gaze away from the Covered Man and shifted it to the fire. He picked up a log near his feet and threw it onto the blaze. "Oh, I am not completely sure, to be honest. We were hiding underground at the time."

The Covered Man leaned back and replaced his hand on his crude spoon. He seemed satisfied by the answer.

He swirled the spoon through the stew once and lifted the cracked plate to where his lips should be and tilted it. The contents passed through the fabric of his suit effortlessly, as if it didn't even exist.

Rays perked up, "Wow! That's one heck of a getup you have there, Mister Trash Bag. I'll bet you have a lot of tricks in that suit. Were you in the military or something?"

The Covered Man didn't seem to hear the question and continued to scoop the meager food to the space where his mouth should be.

As the meal wound down, Rays and Linda gathered up the dirty dishes and placed them in a nearby metal bin. Their task nearing completion, Linda turned back to their guest. "Why don't you help us?" She picked up a piece of cloth from a nearby crate and wiped her hands on it. "With all the gear you traded, you didn't get it all from scrounging, did you?"

The Covered Man just stared at the dying embers of the fire in front of him, waiting for the next inevitable question.

"Help us clean up Blac Arth," she said.

The rest of them perked up, as if they felt bright sunshine for the first time after a long, dark winter. "With your help, I am certain we could make this place livable again."

"What's in it for me?"

The gloom that covered the settlers moments before returned with a vengeance.

Linda put her hands on her hips. "The knowledge that you helped make this world a brighter place. That you cleared away the cobwebs of misery to allow the world to live again."

The Covered Man regretted his decision to stay for the meal. "World's nothing but misery. Misery, deceit, and false hopes." He stood up. "Avoid seeking out problems, unless we can deal."

Linda stood with her mouth open, aghast by the bluntness of the stranger. Tears welled up in Kristine's eyes.

Joshua spoke up from the corner. His arms folded, his gray eyes bore into The Covered Man. "We can keep you supplied with parts and fuel for your car."

Linda spoke through a cracked voice. "If you don't help us, someday we won't be here to trade with anymore."

"There are others to trade with."

Linda broke into sobbing, desperation winding its tentacles into her mind, and Rays stood to comfort her.

Manny said, "After we shared our food with you."

"Kept my part of the bargain. Helped you move stuff. Traded in good faith."

Manny opened his mouth to add something, then closed it.

David had a look of defeat on his grizzled face. He reached down to retrieve a case that rested on the floor next to him. Placing it on his lap, he opened it and pulled out a finely crafted fiddle and bow with one hand, then replaced the case on the floor.

When the bow struck the strings of the fiddle, a melody of sorrow and despair emitted from the strings, reflecting the mood of the last six people of Blac Arth. Sadness engulfed the room as the beautiful sounds wound their way around the group like a siren's song, luring them to their own demise.

The pounding on the door increased in volume. Rays hugged Linda and Kristine tight and tried to assure them everything would be all right. The Covered Man knew it was a lie; to keep them from committing suicide, most likely. Manny took a heavy swig from a bottle and stared at the floor. Joshua stood in the shadows of the room. The Covered Man felt the man's eyes upon him.

The tune took on an even darker tone. The Covered Man snapped out of his thoughts. It was one he recognized from long ago. Images, drudged up from the bottom of a muck-filled pit, rose to the surface. Memories of children playing, new toys, and the illusion of youth. Family gatherings, couples dancing, and people happy to be alive. Things like this were now dead in this world. Maybe he was the only one who remembered why.

He knew what he needed to do.

He leaned back and fell asleep.

The six remaining residents of Blac Arth woke up to the smell of burning flesh. Rays could tell it was still dark out from the skylight. He quickly made sure his family was all right. Joshua looked over them all to see if he could determine where the smell was coming from. The black car was still there, but the Covered Man was nowhere to be seen.

Joshua rushed to the smaller door and found the bolt locks open. He threw open the door, Manny behind him with his rifle unslung and ready, and David with a shotgun. In the middle of the street, a stone's throw away, there was a blaze that burned higher than the Covered Man standing next to it, keeping the darkness of the early morning at bay.

As they watched, he threw a sickly looking body on the pyre. A pile of at least four others lay nearby.

Joshua spoke first. "Busy night, huh?"

"No."

Rays added, "You decided to stay and help us."

"Not helping. Cleaning off car parking space."

The citizens of Blac Arth smiled.

The Covered Man strode over to corpse pile and picked up another to toss on the blaze. He stared at the six people watching his every move. "Babblers usually have some kind of den. Know where that is?"

The Blac Arthers turned toward Manny. "Yeah. I know. Once you get past the train tracks south of here, things get progressively worse. About a block and half on the right side of the road in their encampment. But if you go near that place, you're crazy. Must be fifty of them in there at least."

"Got a shotgun? Shells?"

David tossed his weapon to the Covered Man. "If you can get rid of the babblers, you can have it, stranger. I have a few spares."

The Covered Man walked past them into The Shop, picked up a hacksaw from Joshua's workbench, and placed the blade against the barrel. After only a few cuts, he set the saw down and grasped the barrel in one hand and the stock in the other, then broke the sawed-off part away.

He held it up like a new-born babe and said, "Groovy."

The residents of Blac Arth gazed at him in befuddlement.

Rays ran his hand over his face. "Uh. Yeah. Looks good."

The Covered Man placed the sawed-off in his previously empty holster. "Never mind."

Rays said, "Who would have thought how you dress wasn't the oddest thing about you."

The sun had almost reached its zenith when the small group of Blac Arthers crossed the train tracks to the south of the settlement, leading into the infested ruins. The Covered Man led the way, Manny by his side to point out areas to avoid.

Behind them trailed Rays and Kristine, who helped each other haul a hand truck with a blue barrel strapped to it, struggling with its weight.

The brick building on the left had all its glass broken from its from windows and only a few flakes of its white paint still clung onto the brickwork underneath. Across the street, a lone wooden wall stood, all that remained of a store that had burned to the ground so long ago not even any of the ash remained.

Manny said, "Okay, we need to be as quiet as possible. It's midday, and we only have about a block to go. But babblers and worse live in these ruins."

Rays used his free hand to wipe beads of sweat from his brow. "Easy for you to say. You aren't hauling this thing. It's heavy."

Manny replied, "Not my idea. His." He nodded at the Covered Man.

"Could have at least brought the car," Rays mumbled.

"Rays, you know better than that. The sound of a vehicle alerts anything living in these ruins. Then if it stopped?"

Rays pushed the hand truck over a difficult crack in the pavement, "Everything here would come and find out what happened. Yeah. Yeah. Let's just hurry."

The small group continued, only taking about fifty steps before Manny stopped them again. "Something's watching us."

Kristine scanned the rooftops but saw nothing.

Manny raised his rifle to his chin. "Not sure where, but I can feel it."

The Covered Man withdrew the combat knife from his belt. "Wait here," he said as we set out toward a red brick building. The side facing the street only stood about twenty feet wide with two doorways set into it, both now devoid of doors. As the Covered Man stood facing the building, Rays said, "When he gets killed, we need to hightail it as fast as we can back north."

As if in response, the three of them stepped away from the barrel and retreated a few paces back the way they came.

Moments passed. As they watched the unmoving stranger, a soft metal pinging broke the silence. The Covered Man was tapping his blade against the metal parts of his belt.

Rays shook his head. "What in the world?"

Manny squeezed the bridge of his nose as he understood the stranger's intentions. "That guy's crazy."

No sooner did the words leave his lips than a ten-foot, greenish, millipede-shaped thing sprung from the left-hand door of the structure. The Covered Man snatched the monstrosity from the air as it tried to coil around him. Several tongue-like appendages uncoiled from its head and lashed out.

Rays drew both of his pistols and placed himself between the combatants and his daughter.

Manny held a hand in front of him. "Don't shoot. You'll bring every unholy thing in these ruins down on top of us."

"Are you kidding? That thing is going to eat Mister Goggles for lunch, and we're next!"

They watched as the Covered Man held the head of the millipede away from his body and sunk his knife deep into his foe. The thing used its tail like a flail, beating it against him.

The Covered Man retained his grip on the beast and pinned it to the broken asphalt road. His blade struck again and again. Several of the tongues flopped around on the street nearby like fish out of water. Finally, the rest of the monster went limp, its life essence leaking out multiple stab wounds.

The Covered Man stood up, retrieved a rag from his belt, and wiped his knife clean before sheathing it.

Rays stood, gasping in disbelief. "That was amazing!"

Manny added, "You must be superhuman to take on a ruins crawler by yourself. I heard all of you died in the BeforeTimes."

As the Covered Man strode back towards them, he said, "Hide."

Rays replaced the pistols into his holsters. "Wait a minute. You're a super! Why didn't you say something?"

The Covered Man strode over to the blue barrel and said, "Never asked." He then hoisted it onto his shoulder.

Kristine's mouth went agape. "Hey! If you can carry that, why did you make us haul it all this way?"

"Give you something to do," he said as he walked down the street to a structure with metal siding. Again he said, "Hide. Eyes open. Probably have to use gunfire. Noise."

Kristine stared after him for a moment. Then Rays beckoned her to follow them into the structure the ruins crawler just came from. Manny held his rifle at the ready. Rays and Kristine followed.

The Covered Man stood next to the metal-sided building and pulled the plug from the barrel. Walking along its northern edge, he poured liquid contents onto the wall. The entire western edge of the building used to be some kind of loading dock, but had collapsed. There would be no escaping that way, only to the east.

The last of the liquid left the barrel and the Covered Man turned back to where the Blac Arthers were and set it on the street, careful to keep the noise to a minimum.

Manny dug a lighter out of his pocket. "Here. You will need this to light it."

The Covered Man shook his head, and removed a small, finger sized device from one of his belt pouches. "Thermal."

The device flew through the air and landed at the side of the building. For a second, nothing happened. The next, a white flash glowing like a miniature sun, enveloped the area, forcing all of them to look away. A silent wave of blistering heat washed over them.

After a few moments, the inhabitants of the brick building felt the heat subside and unshielded their faces. The whole side of the metal building was aflame. Nothing was left of the siding but melted slag.

The grass. A nearby tree. All of it belched smoke skyward. Flame devoured everything it danced along. Numerous babbling and gibbering voices rose to a deafening roar.

Readying his weapon in one hand, and holding two shells in the other, the Covered Man stood directly in front of the doorway.

Babblers coated with flame flooded out of the door. A single blast from the sawed-off tore into the flesh of multiple misshapen once-humans. A half dozen of them crumpled to the ground. Waiting for a moment to let more babblers flee the flames, he let loose with the second barrel. Blood spattered the metal siding as the babblers fell to the ground.

Screams turned from fear to rage as their meager minds deduced they were under attack. Their long nails tore at one another in madness to get out of the building and rip apart their attacker.

The Covered Man back up a few steps to give himself some space to reload. The wave of bodies pushed their way out of the door.

Ejecting the two shells, he shoved the two he had ready in to replace them. One of the babblers grabbed the barrel, trying to tear the weapon away. The sawed-off kicked and spit fire, and the babbler's hand disintegrated along with the side of its head.

The Covered Man cursed. He hoped each shell would dwindle the enemy's numbers as much as they could. Firing off his last shell, he backed up yet again to prepare to face the wall of twisted humans hand to hand.

More shots fired off. Manny picking off stragglers with his rifle, Rays stood outside the two-doored building, firing both of his pistols. Kristine off to one side of him with her oversized pistol. The Covered Man waded into gunfire. He smashed a fist into one of the babblers, sending it tumbling to the ground and snapping its neck. He grabbed two more and slammed them together, knocking both unconscious.

A flood of broken, twisted living things broke on the granite-like edifice in goggles. Fists, elbow, and knee strikes cracked bones and tore the muscles of his opponents.

The broken section of street drank of the fluids and organs of the fallen, even as their skin scorched black with flame.

As bodies piled up, the rest of the babblers broke and ran. Some fell along the way, dying from their burns.

The Blac Arthers watched with amazement at the super from a time they could not even remember, standing with his fists still clenched amidst a pile of bodies that reached halfway up his calves.

Crouching, he tossed the bodies aside like broken toys. He displayed no emotion about things once human, just focused on the task at hand. He stopped when he discovered what he was looking for, surviving babblers.

One began to wriggle around, trying to free itself from the bodies of its companions piled on top of it. Another moaned, revealing it just began to stir from unconsciousness.

Reaching down to tear up a chunk of asphalt, he raised it above his head and, with all of his might, brought it down on the head of the babbler trying to free itself. Everything above its neck was crushed to a red paste, and bits of brain and blood leaked from the seam of the asphalt chunk onto the road.

When the second babbler finally won the battle to open its eyes, it spied the figure standing over it, a long shriek burst forth from its throat. Foam flecked its lips, dry and cracked as the road it lay upon.

Crooked teeth tried to tear away the Covered Man's boot, only to have him place the same boot on its ribcage. With a shift of weight and a crunch like stepping on a cockroach, he crushed its ribcage under his foot.

The three Blac Arthers watched with horror. The babblers terrified The Shop for over a year, but something about how callously the man in the black suit snuffed them out was even more frightening.

He turned to face the three of them, and they felt their blood turn cold. Sweat coated their palms and kept their fingers on the triggers of their weapons as the Covered Man strode past them, beginning the trek back to Blac Arth. Manny, Rays, and Kristine looked at each other briefly, without saying a word, they followed.

With their focus on the Stranger, and minds staggered of what they just encountered, none of them noticed the two raiders, brought by the sound of gunfire. From around the corner of an of an abandoned building, they watched the group head northward for a bit. Then with a silent nod to each other, they ran south to report to Fappa Jack.

By the time the four of them returned to the area of The Shop and The Box, the pyre had all but burned itself out. Joshua stood there, poking at the hot embers with a stick, and watched as the sparks leap upward into the air.

The Covered Man walked past and Joshua spoke without looking up from the embers, "Good Hunting?"

There was no answer but the door of the Box flying open. "Honey! You're back!" Linda ran out and threw her arms around her husband, kissing him. Rays hugged and kissed her back.

After a moment, she let go of him and hugged Kristine. "You keeping these boys alive, dear?"

Kristine smiled, but she stared off to the side, the carnage she witnessed still burning in her mind, and didn't reply.

"Hey, Joshua. Did you know Trash Bag is a super?"

Joshua glanced from Rays to the Covered Man, "Yeah?"

"Yeah! Damnest thing I ever saw. Not only did he take out a ruins crawler with a knife, but he took the brunt of the attack of all the babblers. All. Of. Them. More than twenty, at least."

Joshua asked Manny, "Is that true? By himself?"

Manny's skin turned a shade paler. "Yeah."

Joshua poked the embers one last time, "The babbler nest is gone then?"

"Yeah." The Covered Man loaded the final round into his pistol and replaced it on his belt. Then pulled a rag and a small vial from his belt, and began cleaning the sawed off.

Joshua took a half smoked cigar from the chest pocket of his jumpsuit, put it in his mouth, then used the red hot ember on the end of the stick to re-light it. Exhaling a cloud of smoke into the air, he said, "So, mister super. What is the plan now? With the nest gone, the stragglers shouldn't be too much of a problem."

Linda asked, "What else do we have to do to make this place safer?"

Everyone but the Covered Man looked at Manny who said, "Jack."

Joshua nodded, "Tribute time is fast approaching."

Manny just stared at the rifle in his hands, "How to stop all those raiders."

As the Covered Man finished cleaning the sawed-off, he replaced it on his belt. Removing his knife, he wiped it down once quickly with the rag, "World's a cold, dark place. Surviving means you have to be colder. Darker."

Replacing all of his gear on his belt, he made one last check of everything, then went into The Shop to retrieve more ammunition, leaving the other Blac Arthers to ponder his meaning.

A few babbler free nights passed, allowing the citizens of Blac Arth to sleep better than they had in a while. The Covered Man began dragging or pushing old vehicles to The Box to begin creating a makeshift wall.

The greatest find was a semi-trailer about two hundred yards south down 'the 78'. It took him almost all afternoon to pull it back, like Hercules performing one of his great Labors. Joshua lit up his welder and got to work. The trailer itself had long been looted. But the components would go far to help them protect the rebuilding of their settlement.

As they dismantled it, David did little to help, as his age did not lend him the strength of the younger settlers. Instead, he retrieved his fiddle from The Shop and sat on the roof of The Box. Linda and Kristine sat nearby, each with a rifle to keep watch. Placing bow to string, he played an upbeat tune and even hummed along where the words of the song used to be. His playing lifted everyone's spirits and the work somehow became easier.

After a while, Linda stood up, looking off to the north, "Visitors coming! Looks like some of Sike and his bunch."
Joshua lifted the visor of his welding mask just as three men crossed 'the 78', each armed with a rifle. None of them look like they have washed or bathed in days. Joshua pulled a cigar from his pocket and lit it from the torch before dousing its flame.

For a moment they stopped and everyone just stared at each other. They glanced from the partly-disassembled trailer to the Covered Man, Joshua, Rays, David—still playing a tune—and to those on the roof.

Joshua spoke first. "Afternoon, Sike. Javier. Dor." He lowered the blowtorch, took the cigar out of his mouth, and blew out a long stream of smoke, as one would do long ago on a lazy summer afternoon after cooking out on the grill and waiting for the evening with nothing to do.

Javier, a man with dark hair and the most trimmed beard of the bunch, although that was not saying much, found his voice first. "What the heck is going on, Joshua?"

"Why, rebuilding Blac Arth, of course." He replaced the cigar in his mouth. "What does it look like?"

Javier's look of bewilderment soon changed into one of amazement. "No way."

Joshua mimicked the grin. "Mmm hmm."

Then Sike found his voice. His rawhide jacket had slight fringe on it. The wide brimmed black hat covered his straight black hair and reddish tinted skin. He spoke to Joshua, but his eyes remained on the Covered Man. "We saw the pillar of smoke a while back and caught the whiff of burning skin. We thought for sure we'd find the lot of you finally done in. Instead, we find you rebuilding the place."

Rays spoke up. "Yeah. Well, the babblers were a'babblin' something fierce, so we had to do something about it." He pointed at the days old remains of the bonfire, now just a pile of ash and bits of bone.

Javier shook his head. "We expected to find you dead, and it looks like you are preparing for a… an… I don't know what." He thought for a moment to drudge up a long forgotten word from his memory. "A festival!"

Sike said, "You realize the moment Jack gets a whiff of this, he will be on this place like ants on dropped food. He will tear this place out from underneath you." He spat on the ground, as if what he just said filled his throat with bile.

Rays smiled even wider. "Yeah. But get this, our newest resident is a super!"

Sike sneered. "Rays, you are so full of it. The supers are all dead. They were all fools who screwed us over and then killed themselves."

"Oh yeah, mister smarty Sike? This guy""—Rays pointed at the Covered Man— "pulled that old trailer here all by himself!"

The three men looked at each other and then at the Covered Man, who stood like an unmovable mountain.

Sike shouted, "Hey! Hey, David. Stop playing for a second."

The old man stopped and set the fiddle in his lap. Peering over the edge of the roof, he replied, "Yeah, Sike. What you want? How's the missus?"

"Oh uh, she's fine. Thanks for askin'. Is what Rays sayin' true? You always were the smartest one of this bunch."

If David smiled, it couldn't have been seen through his thick, gray grizzled beard. He raised the fiddle back to his chin and shouted back before he resumed playing, "Every word."

Sike, Javier, and Dor looked at each other again for a moment and strolled forward. Sike said, "So uh, mister super-type, what's your plan here? What were the BeforeTimes like?"

Rays chuckled to himself and said, "Don't even try. He talks less than Joshua."

Javier asked, "Is that even possible?"

"All right, enough," Joshua said. "We have to get back to work if we want to get this truck disassembled while we still have daylight." To punctuate his point, he removed the cigar from his mouth, crushed it out on the steel of the trailer, then replaced it in the breast pocket of his jumpsuit. The torch flared back into life, as life flared into the eyes of the three newcomers.

Sike said, "Mind if we, uh, stay and watch a while? We have plenty of time before we get back to the families." They lied as they looked up at the evening sky.

Linda shouted down to them, "Sure, you can come up here and help us keep watch!"

As the three men made their way onto the roof, the Covered Man grabbed the next section Joshua planned to cut away. He held it steady, and the work continued.

⚶

By the time the long shadows of evening disappeared into night, the trailer had been completely dismantled. With the trailer bottom, two long sides, and the front, they erected a thirteen-foot wall, closing the entrances of The Box and The Shop. This gave them a large rectangular courtyard. The door that allowed access to the trailer lay nearby.

It needed some modification, but the Covered Man had to wait for the residents of Blac Arth to rest and eat. He stood on the roof of The Box and kept a lookout for trouble while they sat around a campfire below. It was a good sign that the sun had set and nothing attacked, but he had not lived as long as he had by surrendering to hopes and wishes.

Kristine climbed the ladder to the roof and approached him. "Aren't you coming down to eat?"

"No."

Kristine bit her lip for a moment, then said, "Sike has a bottle of bourbon, or something similar, and David is going to be pulling out the fiddle again soon."

The Covered Man looked from his car, sitting in the shop, to the beckoning horizon. He spoke loud enough that everyone below could hear him clearly. "If the gate isn't finished soon, none of that will matter. The dead don't need bourbon or fiddles."

Disappointment filled Kristine's eyes and the sounds of happiness below dwindled, and he knew his message had sunk in. As Kristine returned to the ladder to climb down, the hurried clanking of plates and cups indicated a hasty meal. The Covered Man gazed at the setting sun. He knew if he stayed there, he would die there.

By the time Joshua welded the makeshift gate into its final resting place, the sun was almost behind the trees. Linda and Kristine leaned on their shovels in exhaustion. The Covered Man had a few pyrotechnics in his trunk, which they buried alongside 'The 78'.

Sooner or later, attackers would come, and anything they could do to defend their home would hopefully turn the tide someday.

Joshua turned off the blow torch, took off the welder's helmet, and threw it on the ground. He looked exhausted.

Rays leaned against the newly built wall and wiped the sweat from his brow. Sike and Javier walked over to a bench and sat down to rest. Shortly after they ate, they sent Dor back to their families to report the goings on in the growing settlement of Blac Arth.

Javier stared at the ground. "Damn. I thought scavenging was hard work. Trash Bag, you are a harsh guy to work for."

The Covered Man just grabbed Rays' rifle and walked to the ladder of The Box.

As the last remnants of the sun slipped behind the trees, the silence of the infant night began to be interrupted by the cries of animals. The gibbering cries of babblers could be heard, but they were few and far off in the distance to be anything more than a minor concern. A bonfire roared by the gate; a beacon to the rest of the world, and a warning for the enemies of the infant settlement.

Somewhere off in the distance, they heard the roars of multiple engines approaching.

Sike stood on the roof of The Box with a rifle held in both of his hands. Next to him stood the Covered Man, just staring off southward into the evening gloom

Sike said in a low voice, "Hope whatever plan you had, it's a good one. They're coming."

Manny and Linda were climbing to the roof of The Box, while Rays, Joshua and Javier stayed on the ground to stay close to anything that needed repairing.

His pistols hung on his belt and he leaned heavily on a hockey stick

Rays stood with his pistols on his belt. His right hand holding onto a hockey stick with a jagged saw blade screwed to the end of it. "I'm ready to puck somebody up."

Javier just shook his head, "That's awful. You must be the most optimistic person after the fall of humanity."

Rays replied, "A cannibal ate an optimist once. They couldn't quite keep him down."

Javier asked Joshua, "Can't we just leave him outside of the wall?"

Joshua just shrugged while Rays smiled to himself.

Sike raised the rifle to his eye, searching for any hint of movement. As Manny reached the top of the roof, followed by Linda, he unslung his rifle and asked Sike, "Are they coming? Is Fappa Jack with them?"

"They are coming. But unsure who will be leading them. It might just be Megmas."

Manny said to Linda who was just reaching the top rungs of the ladder, "Have Rays light 'em up."

Linda, turned and faced the courtyard below them, "Light 'em up, dear!"

Rays nodded up at his wife and then turned to Joshua and Javier. "I am not sure how our generator is going to take all this."

"I know. A night or two of this and our fuel will be gone. Not to mention the wear and tear on the generator." He readjusted the grip on the crudely forged sword in his hand, obviously more accustomed to using a welder's torch than a weapon.
Javier just nodded and once again checked the sights on the pistol he carried.

Rays rested the hockey stick he carried against the wall. picked up a small box with a thick black wire connected to it. On one side of the box was a switch. He said so quietly the only one who heard was his old friend Joshua, "Let's do this." And he flipped the switch.

A series of lights illuminated along the top of the wall, some of them flickered and went dark, either the bulbs or the wiring giving up the ghost.

On the roof, the Covered Man looked out at the ocean of headlights that now lit up the night. At least twenty cars and the same number of motorcycles were pulling up along 'the 78'. They were stopping about a dozen or two paces from the wall just at the edge of the illumination.

Of the vehicles that could be seen, the light revealed most were makeshift buckets of parts. They began revving their engines in unison.

While the motors belched out their noise and smoke, Joshua climbed the ladder to the roof of The Box, "Hey!" Joshua shouted.

As the engines continued with their cacophony of noise, he yelled again, this time waving his arms, "Hey! Jack! Cut it, will yah? We all know how this goes."

With that, all the engines slowly sputtered and stopped. They heard a few car doors open and slam in the still of the evening. A tall muscular man stepped into the glow of the headlights of one of the cars. It was impossible to make out details, but he had a few pieces of plastic tied to him as armor, and a lot of feathers strapped to his arms, giving him the appearance of a huge bird.

"Hey, Joshua." A calm voice said. A feather coated arm made a sweeping motion at the wall. "What's all this? You trying to keep us out?" Two other figures stood at the edge of the light, one stood a head taller than the Covered Man, the other thin and lithe.

"We are building something solid here, Jack. Maybe a farm. A few animals."

The figure silhouetted by the headlights laughed and multiple other voices laughed along with. "Here? Are you kidding? With *her* to the northwest and Mad Town a short distance away?" He looked around at the dead babblers that littered the ground. "You will be dead by year's end. Even with us in the way." After a shout pause he asked, "Is, uh, is Manny still with you?"

All turned. Manny stood on the far side of the roof, trying to look inconspicuous. "Yeah, Jack. I'm here."

"Why don't you come back and ride with us again, Manny. You always were a good shot." A few chuckles were heard from the shapes in the darkness. "We could use your skills."

"Jack, I gave all that up. I don't want to take things anymore. I need something a bit more stable."

"So be it. Prepare to die with these fools. We will *take* our tribute now, then."

Joshua bit his lip. "Tribute? It's a bit early for that isn't it? Most of our resources went to build the fortification."

Javier shouted from behind the wall, "Get lost! We don't deal with vermin like you any more!"

The feathered silhouette spoke again. "Vermin? Hear that, he called us vermin." A round of laughter and fake scared sounds rippled through the air.

"Tell you what, since you are just starting out, we will go easy on you. Rays? You there?"

"Yeah."

"I see your daughter on the roof there. She has become quite the ripe cherry to pluck. Give her to us for a night. We promise we won't kill her. We will just *sample* her, and return her tomorrow. That will give you a month to put together a proper tribute for our protection of what lies beyond us."

Linda put herself between Kristine and the view of those out in the darkness.

The Covered Man is the one who replied, "Or you leave."

"What? Who is this, Joshua? A goth owl? Hoot up your own business, owl! Or you will find yourself hanging from this tin barricade with your intestines as a hat." Jack turned back to Joshua," What's your decision? We get her and she has a place to return too? Or we get her and she joins us permanently. What's it going to be?"

The Covered Man walked out onto the section of the wall that was the bottom of the trailer. The sound of many guns cocking echoed from the street. He said, "Or you leave, Big Bird. Intact or as a feather duster."

Rays said, "We are going to need a trash bag for Mister Trash Bag, I think."

Jack said, "You must have a death wish, Owl." He stretched his arms out wide and paced in a figure eight in front of the headlights. "There are dozens of us, and only one of you. With one command, you will be punctured almost as much as Rays' daughter will be after we kill everyone and take her. Got anything to say before heading to the great beyond?"

"Yeah. Second switch."

"That won't look great on your headstone, but so be—"

Linda threw the second switch and the night lit up from the flash bombs she and Kristine buried under in the dirt along the sides of the road earlier that day. The blast of white fire engulfed everything outside the metal walls and blinded everyone but the goggle-wearing Covered Man.

As the raiders ran around with clothes and hair ablaze, The Covered Man jumped to the ground and waded into the wall of fire; the heat burned his skin, but the suit protected him from any true injury. It would be as if he had a sunburn for a few days until his enhanced healing got him back to normal. He had been losing his powers steadily over the past months, but no time to dwell on that now.

The Covered Man already finished the first clip in his pistol and was replacing it when another raider ran towards him through the flames a crude shotgun leveled at him.

Before the raider could pull the trigger, the heat caused the gunpowder to ignite, destroying the gun and removing two fingers from her right hand.

Snapping the new clip into place, he fired at the approaching opponent, one bullet between the eyes put her on the ground.

"*Owl!*"

Standing on the burning wreckage of a car stood Fappa Jack. The feathers had completely burned away and the leather pieces of his armor were charred and cracked. He held a knife in one hand and a sword with a jagged blade in the other. "I am going to use your testicles as earrings! You hear me? Earrings!"

The Covered Man pointed the pistol at him, and fired. The wisps of heat from the flames obscured Fappa Jack to cause the metal projectile to miss. Fappa Jack dropped behind the car to hide. "No. No. No. You don't get a crack at me, Owl. You never will! Instead, you will meet my War Chugger, Bum Bag! I promised him he could rape your corpse!"

The car was pushed over. There was no sign of Fappa Jack, in his place was the raider that stood a head taller than the Covered Man. He wore only an S&M hood, chaps tied to his legs with numerous spikes pushing through it, and heavy boots. He wielded a thick wooden pole, which was also lined with spikes and nails.

Bum Bag lifted the pole over his head and flexed his muscles. "You're gonna be Bum Bag's bum bag!"

45

The Covered Man outstretched his arm to put a well-placed bullet into his opponent's head when the crack of a whip pierced the air and something struck his hand, making him drop his gun.

It was the other goon that stood by Fappa Jack in the headlights earlier. His lithe, muscular form had ebony skin where not a hair follicle could be seen. A full clown mask with no pigment left on it covered his head. He wore leather pants with boots that came up to his knees. A sword with a slight curve to it hung from his belt. In his right hand he held a rawhide whip laced with rusty nails.

Before the Covered Man had a chance to pick up the pistol, Bum Bag charged at him, the spiked pole lifted overhead ready to be brought down on his opponent. The Covered Man dodged backwards as the pole descended, but a few of the longer spikes tore across his flesh, leaving thin red trails for a moment before the suit swallowed them up.

The Covered Man kept his eye on the spiked pole. As long as Bum Bag had that, he had the longer reach, and the advantage. Bum Bag swung high, attempting to knock the Covered Man's head from his shoulders. The Covered Man grabbed Bum Bag's closest arm and sent a few well-placed knees to his opponent's stomach to get him to drop the weapon.

It was like striking a wall. Bum Bag slammed his elbow into the side of the Covered Man's face, causing him to stagger backwards. The Covered Man shook his head. For a human, Bum Bag was exceptionally fast and strong. Maybe some kind of drug? Was the deterioration of his powers worse than he thought? The Covered Man realized he had a real fight on his hands.

Bum Bag squared off against his opponent, looking for an opening. "Smell your death Goggles? I am undefeated! We hold this area under our thumb and always will. Long after you are a memory!"

The Covered Man swung high with his right fist. Bum Bag raised the spiked pole to block it, so he swept out with his left foot and kicked Bum Bag in the shin, making him stumble. As the Covered Man lunged to grab the weapon away, the car behind him exploded. Again, the heat could not penetrate his suit, but the blast was enough to knock him to his knees.

Despite sections of his skin seared in the heat, Bum Bag saw his opening and swung his weapon in a wide arc. It stuck the Covered Man across his back.

The spike in the pole held in place for a moment before Bum Bag ripped it free. As the Covered Man struggled to get to his feet, Bum Bag brought the non-spiked end of the pole across his forehead, knocking him prone.

As the Covered Man lay on the ground, Bum Bag used his sandaled foot to kick him in the ribs. The Covered Man rolled onto his side so the blows would connect square in the stomach. Bum Bag laughed with maniacal glee. "So much for the champion of Black Arth!"

Fappa Jack shouted, "This the best you got? You better wheel your daughter's ass out first! We might just let you live!" The rest of the raiders that were still alive laughed, ready for any payback.

Fappa Jack turned to Bum Bag. "End this. We need to put this fool's head on a pike then claim our succulent prize." He turned to his clown-masked lieutenant. "Megmas, check what vehicles still are operational. We will tear down this wall for scrap and drag it back to Horb."

Both Bum Bag and Megmas nodded to show allegiance to their leader. Megmas replaced the whip on his belt and ran off. Bum Bag prepared one final stomp on the Covered Man's neck, only to have the prone figure strike up with a knife into the back of his knee, the tip of the blade poking out from between Bum Bag's left kneecap and tibia. The scream was long and painful.

Letting go of the knife, the Covered Man kicked his heel into Bum Bag's wounded knee with all his might. Bum Bag planted the base of the pole on the ground to keep on his feet. His free hand tried to reach around and grab the knife, but any shifting of his weight made his leg burn with fire.

Struggling to his feet, the Covered Man slammed his fist into Bum Bag's head three times, just enough to get him to let go of the spiked pole. The Covered Man grabbed it before it hit the ground and kicked at Bum Bag's wounded knee again, this time sending Bum Bag to the ground.

The Covered Man turned and looked at Fappa Jack. "Leave." He spun the pole and Bum Bag cried out as the Covered Man struck him in the forehead with a sickening, cracking sound. Some of the spikes drove so far into his head, they could no longer be seen.

Bum Bag's body went limp, the spiked Pole lodged deep in his skull.

Fappa Jack screamed, "No!"

The Covered Man held a hand against a bruised rib as he walked through the wreckage toward Fappa Jack. The raider hastily climbed onto a new vehicle, using the passenger side window as a seat. A lot of the fires were already burning low.

Fappa Jack slapped the hood of the car twice. "Back to the base to regroup!"

Those that remained helped the wounded into the vehicles and sped off into the night.

Rays cheered, "We did it!" The rest of the settlers of Black Arth cheered. All except the Covered Man, who limped toward Fappa Jack. He managed a few more hops before he collapsed from the pain, and he sprawled out on the ground and passed out.

The Covered Man awoke on a cot in The Shop, and he tried to sit up. His ribs ached like fire. The room spun.

He got lucky. The fury of the attack of Bum Bag caught him off guard. He almost lost his life. If Fappa Jack did not stop to gloat, to give him a second wind he would be dead. The Covered Man groaned as he tried to get up. The pain in his side tore through him, and he fell back limp onto the cot.

Kristine shrieked at the top of her lungs, "Joshua! Hey, Joshua! He's awake!"

The Covered Man looked over at her. If anyone else was around, he could not see them. The pain too great to look around. Again, he wondered why his powers were fading.

"For a super, you really got your butt kicked."

"Still alive. Other guy isn't."

"That's for sure. You split his head like you split a log. It was great!"

Joshua and Sike entered The Shop. Sike said, "Mornin', Trash Bag, Killer of Bum Bag. Cannot believe we saw the last of him. Damndest fight I ever saw." He basked in the glory of the memory for a moment and then looked the Covered Man over. "You look like death in a death ray, friend."

The Covered Man tried to get up again, but the world still spun, and he laid back on the cot. He brought his forearm up and rested it on his forehead to stop the world from moving.

Sike said, "You shouldn't try to get up, Mister Bag. We managed before you showed. We can manage now. Dor returned with our families. The wall will be fully repaired by the end of the day and we looted the charred raiders. We even salvaged one of Jack's vehicles and got it working, a truck!" The Blac Arthers beamed at their accomplishments.

The Covered Man ignored their accomplishments, "Out long?"

"Day. Day and a half. It's almost noon. From the beating you took, we figured you would be out longer. But we…"

The Covered Man forced himself to sit up and swung one of his feet on the ground. He wobbled as if he would fall to the floor. The three that watched him stuck out their arms to steady him, but when they were certain he would remain upright, they withdrew. They were rewarded for their offer to help by the Covered Man vomiting through his mask onto the floor, streaks of crimson running through it.

Kristine said, "I am not sure what is more disturbing, that you hurled, or you did it through that mask that didn't move."

Joshua said, "Where did you ever get that outfit, anyway?"

The Covered Man didn't answer; instead, he grasped Sike's shoulder and pulled himself to his feet. "Already lost a day. Need to get ready for the return."

"They didn't return last night. We were sure Jack would return, but he didn't."

The Covered Man snapped at them, "They will!" His whole side blazed with pain as he headed toward the door leading to the outside.

The three of them followed the Covered Man, curious what someone who could barely walk would do. As he walked outside, the Covered Man saw the truck they salvaged and got running. Rays and Linda were there. Linda sat in the driver's seat while Rays tinkered with the engine. He managed a side glance at the Covered Man. "If it isn't the Bum Bag Buster." He turned the ratchet on one of the hoses connected to the engine. "Glad to see you back amongst the living."

"How many more cars are there like this?"

Rays stood up and looked puzzled. "This is the only one that wasn't charred to a crisp. But there are maybe four more wrecks out there. But we already stripped them for parts."

"Open the gate."

"But wha—"

"Open the gate!"

Rays shouted up to the roof. "Hey Manny! You up there?"

Manny came from the north side of the roof. "Yeah?"

"Can you pull the gate open?"

Manny nodded and slung the rifle over his shoulder. Picking up the ropes that connected to the gate, he gave them a few hard pulls, raising the gate enough for the Covered Man to limp through. The area where 'the 78' and Canal Street connected was still charred black from the thermite charges they rigged up. The burned remains of four cars and two motorcycles remained. In the empty lot across the street, one could see the remains of a bonfire. A few human bones poked out of the ashes.

The Covered Man went to the nearest car and strained as he pushed it to the junction. His leg buckled a bit before he flipped it on its side, like he did with the trailer of the truck. Javier and Dor ran over to attempt to help him move another of the other ruined cars next to the first. Soon all four of the charred vehicles became part of the growing barricade around their home. By the time he finished moving the cars, the Covered Man collapsed on the ground, his back against the car he just stood on end.

Manny stood on the roof of The Box, and shouted down at him, "Hey, Bag Buster! You okay?"

The Covered Man didn't answer. He just got to his feet and retrieved one of the abandoned motorcycles. Then he jammed it against one of the upright cars and set the other side in the dirt for support. He did the same with the other motorcycle.

Javier ran his fingers through his hair, "Looks like the beginnings of another barrier."

"Exactly."

"What are you going to do? Build that all around Blac Arth?"

"Yeah."

"That's an ambitious project."

"Only way to be free from the Fappa Jack's of the world is to be self-reliant. Means room to grow is needed."

"How…?"

"Take it. Defend it."

"Where are we going to get enough scrap to build such a thing?"

"Fappa Jack."

52

Linda crouched on the roof of an abandoned auto repair building on the edge of the ruins of Horb with binoculars and a rifle. She gazed down the street to Fappa Jack's base. There was some activity as they got ready for a day's scavenging. She called down to the Covered Man in his black car and Rays, Sikes, and Dor in the truck they pieced together. "They are out in front of the building. They must be getting ready to scav."

Rays waved up at her, "Thanks dear. Don't forget to be careful."

"I am up here, my sweet. You have the hard work to do. Wait." She lifted the binoculars to her eyes and squinted through them. "Here they come. Two, no, three of them, and a bike." She crouched down low again to remain hidden.

The Covered Man kept his foot on the gas and when the vehicles raced past, he punched it, emitting a screech from the tires as they pressed against the cracked pavement underneath them.

The black car's engine roared like a demon as it raced to catch up with the vehicles. It pulled alongside the rear most car, a red car. The driver didn't notice them, but the raider in the back seat did. As she pulled her pistol to fire, The Covered Man jerked his wheel hard with one hand and readied the sawed off with the other.

The raider in the passenger seat saw the Covered Man for only a split second before the sawed off discharged, tearing his face to shreds. That was followed by a ton and a half of steel ramming into the side of the red car, causing it to careen off the side of the road and slam into a tree.

The other cars were now alerted to him. The raider on the cycle drew a hand-held crossbow while the vehicle that was mostly rust pulled to his passenger side. The gray car ahead slowed down, forcing the Covered Man to do the same. Both cars had raiders climbing onto their hoods to prepare to make the leap to his car, intent on killing the Covered Man and taking the vehicle as their own.

As the Covered Man snapped the sawed-off open to replace the shells, the raider hanging on the rusty car withdrew a two-foot spear from a holster on his back and leaped onto the black car, howling in delight when he succeeded.

The raider from the gray car also jumped into the space between vehicles, but at the last moment one of his feet slipped. The momentum spun him in space, so he landed with his back to the windshield, cracking both the glass and his back.

With a wild look in his eye, the raider with the spear laughed at his companion's plight.

The Covered Man groaned. He could barely see the road with the raider in the way. He popped two new shells into the sawed-off, but before he snapped it shut. He swerved hard to the left, trying to take out the cyclist, who had now come up on the driver's side. Both vehicles moved along with him, but the cycle fell back a bit, making sure it wouldn't get forced off the road.

As the Covered Man swerved back, the raider on the passenger side was climbing in the window. The raider on his hood maneuvered around so he could smash out the rest of the window.

Snapping the weapon shut, he seized it and fired into the raider on his right. Now missing half of his skull, the raider dropped the short spear on the floor of the car while his lifeless body hung limply out of the passenger side window. Limiting the view in that direction as well.

Not being able to see much in two directions, the Covered Man knew he had to think of a plan, and fast. He pushed the pedal to the floor. He could barely make out the gray car ahead of him, with the raider now hanging onto his hood.

The black car collided solidly with the gray car ahead of it. The raider on the hood clawed at the broken glass of the windshield. He screamed in panic. Unable to maneuver around with a broken back, afraid to let go despite shards of broken glass puncturing his hand.

The rusty car moved alongside the black car once again to let another raider jump on. The Covered Man took his foot off the gas completely so he could lean over and grasp the short spear that rested on the passenger side of the car with his right hand. As he did, the next raider leaped onto the passenger side of the black car and pulled his dead companion from the vehicle.

With a singular thrust, the Covered Man jammed the spear into the neck of the raider on the hood. As he pulled the spear out of the unwanted passenger, a spurt of crimson washed over the front of the car. The source of the new red paint tumbled off onto the cracked pavement below.

Without warning, a crossbow bolt punctured the Covered Man's left shoulder. The motorcycle had pulled up alongside of him again, trying to watch the road and reload the crossbow with little success.

The Covered Man swerved, slamming into the rust car, crushing the legs of both the dead and live raiders hanging off that side. The shock made the live raider let go, tumbling to the ground as they sped along.

The rust driver pulled back alongside so he could grab the body of the raider in the window to get a clear shot at the Covered Man. Having a firm grasp on the dead raider, the driver pulled away. The movement dislodged the body from the window, the driver discarded it like an empty cup.

The cyclist fell back still trying to reload the crossbow.

The Covered Man swung back to strike the rusty car with his own. With every last ounce of his strength, he hurtled the spear into the side of the head of the driver. The rusty car spun out and flipped over a few times, glass and metal flung in every direction.

The Covered Man looked around for the sawed-off and saw that it had ended up on the floor of the passenger side, out of reach. He couldn't afford to take his eyes from the road that long to retrieve it like he did the short spear.

Once again pushing his foot to the floor, he tried to ram the back corner of the gray car. The gray car matched the maneuver causing the black car to just connect with the back bumper. The gray car weaved back and forth a little and pulled alongside the black car.

Focusing on the attacking gray car, he didn't even notice the cyclist pull alongside of him again, crossbow loaded. The cyclist fired directly into the Covered Man's tire on the rear driver's side. The tire shredded, causing him to lose control.

The Covered Man slammed on the brakes to keep from going off the road and into a small creek on the left side of the road. He saved the car from going into the creek, but the front of the car now faced the edge of the road. This meant the sides were facing the road itself, leaving the stationary vehicle an easy target.

Pulling the crossbow bolt from his arm and tossing it aside, he grasped the sawed-off and holstered it as he climbed out of the vehicle. Looking for anything nearby to use as a weapon.

The gray car slammed on the brakes and wheeled around to finish off the wounded vehicle, like a vulture made of metal. The cycle slowed down, and the driver put his foot on the ground to watch the carnage.

As the gray car revved its engine, the Covered Man crouched behind his vehicle. He winced in pain as he did, his injuries of the past few days taking their toll. But he worked hastily to remove the shredded tire from his car.

The cyclist howled in delight as the gray car punched the pedal to the floor, aimed directly at the passenger side of the black car. The Covered Man waited. As gray car got up to maximum speed, the Covered Man leaped onto the hood of his car, the destroyed tire in hand. Like Hercules of old throwing a discus, the Covered Man hurled the tire into the windshield on the oncoming car, smashing it and the driver behind it.

The car swerved and rolled over onto its side, sending parts and metal into the air. Instead of directly colliding with the side of the black car, the rolling vehicle just clipped the front, bending the front panel and fender. It threw the Covered Man to the ground, where the twisted metal remains of the gray car landed on his leg. The Covered Man snarled through gritted teeth.

The cyclist panicked, and not waiting to see if the Covered Man still lived, he got the cycle going and spun about, heading back to the ruins of Horb.

The Covered Man was in no shape to stop him. He couldn't feel his leg. He was certain that the wounds he sustained fighting Bum Bag reopened since he could feel the blood tricking down his forehead; only the tight-fitting goggles kept the blood from pouring into his eyes.

The cyclist roared away as the Covered Man tried to survey his surroundings. The gray car lay on its side, still pinning his leg to the ground. Judging from the stillness, whoever was inside was dead or unconscious. A small trickle of fluid poured from wreckage onto the cracked road.

He tried to lift his head, but his body was not responding. Everything was pain. The world spun, and he felt like he had to vomit again. Fearing a concussion, he forced himself onto his left elbow. The searing pain of his twisted leg tore the cobwebs from his mind.

He knew if the cyclist made it back to Horb, Fappa Jack would be back with an entire group of raiders. With the black car in the same shape he was in, he would be easy prey. Kicking the gray car with his good leg, it rolled off of his leg and into the ditch. Pushing off the cracked asphalt with one hand and grabbing the wheel well with the other to steady himself. With all his might, he pulled himself to a sitting position.

His leg felt like it was being torn from its socket as he made it to a sitting position. He wondered if he should just grab what he could from his car and hide in the bushes, then try to make it back to Black Arth on foot in the dark.

As he turned and grasped the wheel well with his second hand, he put his good foot on the ground and tried to pull himself to his feet. The pain was earth-shattering. He heaved, but nothing was in his stomach to spill onto the ground. He let go of the wheel well and again fell to his back, writhing with such pain he could not even manage a scream.

He lay there, wondering if he should just give up and give in. The cyclist had to be almost back to Horb by now. In his anguish, he lost track of time. He moved his right arm across the pavement, looking for where he dropped the sawed-off. He dared not move his head, afraid the pain would begin again if he moved.

He did not know how long he was on that cracked ground when he heard a vehicle approaching from the direction of Horb. He needed to find some way to defend himself. His mind could barely focus. The blood from his head wound pooled up enough it broke the seal of his goggles and leaked into his left eye, partially blinding him.

His right arm almost worked independently of the rest of him and still searched for something nearby to use for a weapon while the rest of the Covered Man barely moved. The engine of the approaching vehicle pulled up on him and stopped. The engine shut off, and he heard people get out.

"Trash Bag. I am going to rename you Body Bag."

Rays and Joshua grabbed the Covered Man and tried to help him to his feet. As his leg twisted, he grimaced in pain. They half dragged him to the passenger seat of the truck and hoisted him inside. The Covered Man saw the truck pulled two broken cars, like a train of destruction. On top of the front most car lay a motorcycle, another cycle peeked out of the bed of the truck. Despite his pain, he still relaxed a little.

The Covered Man sat and watched as the Blac Arthers looted the bodies in the gray car and hooked up the black car to the back of the wreckage train. Linda sat on the roof of the truck with her rifle, watching toward Horb, while Rays and Joshua worked like ants to disassemble what they could from the raider's vehicles to make them lighter to pull.

Rays finally hopped in the driver seat, setting his toolbox on the floor of the truck. Joshua joined Linda on the hood, and they moved forward. The engine revved and a trail of white smoke came from the front of the hood of the truck, but they moved the train of destruction forward.

Rays grinned at the Covered Man. "How did you live so long without us? You end up on your back more than my ex-wife."

The Covered Man just groaned, "Didn't seek trouble as much." He followed with "Don't burn out axle."

"Not to worry, Body Bag. This engine has been modified by the Rays-o-matic!" He grinned wider and hummed "Time After Time" as they crept forward.

The sun lay directly overhead by the time the wreckage train made it back to Blac Arth. Dor, his wife and Manny helped the Covered Man back to his cot in The Shop and then went back outside. The plan was to unhook the wreckage train and then get back to claim the gray car. Hopefully, before anyone else found it.

Joshua, Rays, Sike, Dor and Manny stood by the exit. They tried to lower their voices, but their agitation allowed what they said to carry farther than intended. Allowing the Covered Man to eavesdrop on what they were saying.

Sikes said, "I wouldn't have believed it if I didn't see it. Blac Arth now has the beginnings of a real settlement. With those ruined vehicles to add to the wall, we now have a real chance of defending this place."

Rays nodded. "Amazing times, aren't they. Whoda thunk it?"

Dor chuckled.

Joshua rubbed his beard stubble. "I am still nervous. With the new people filing in to live here, it's putting great strain on The

Shop's generator. If we don't get another generator soon to help alleviate the strain on this one, or worse. If this one breaks down with no backup..."

Manny said, "We know where to get a few generators. The school right up 'the 14'. I can go..."

Joshua cut him off. "Get that thought out of your head, Manny. You are not going to the school. You are one of the best game trackers here. We need you alive. Without you, a lot of these new people here will end up starving. And you know it."

Sikes added, "Not to mention, disturbing She Who Lives Underneath is tantamount to suicide."

Dor cleared his throat. "If the school is out, how about Manny and me head to CroPlay tomorrow and see if we can find something we can use?"

Manny looked at Joshua and replied, "Sounds good to me."

"We don't have much of a choice," Joshua said, "Fappa Jack to the south, *Her* to the northwest. You will get closer to Madtown, so be extra careful."

The Covered Man heard the door to the outside open, and the men were quiet for a moment. Then Rays said, "Hey, dear." Linda must have entered. "Hey Doc Williamson. It's been a while since you have been through here."

A female voice replied, "Not the easiest place to get to unless you go cross country. All along my route, though, people are all talking about the settlement that has risen from the ashes. Where is he?"

Sikes and Manny both said. "Over there,"

"Over on the cot," Rays said.

The Covered Man felt their eyes on him.

Kristine came in and sat down next to him. "We have to stop meeting like this."

The Covered Man just looked at the ceiling.

He saw a woman holding a leather satchel in one hand, the other hand had planks of wood and some torn strips of cloth.

"This is the guy?" Doc Williamson said to Kristine. "He doesn't look super. He looks like an invalid." She placed the objects on the floor and inspected the Covered Man's wounded leg.

"Yeah. Looks fractured." Shifting her gaze from the Covered Man's leg to his face, she asked, "How does it feel?"

"Great."

Doc Williamson looked over her shoulder at Kristine. "You didn't tell me he was a comedian."

Kristine smiled and shrugged. "Usually he doesn't say anything at all."

Doc Williamson reached into her pocket and retrieved a small container. It had a white lid. The container itself was a translucent brown and half filled with pills.

She called the five men who stood by the door over to her. As they strode over, she twisted the cap off and shook two of the pills into her hand. She motioned for them to hold her patient from the BeforeTime firmly to the cot. The doc twisted the cap back on, pills still in her hand. With her free hand she replaced the container in her pocket, then reached up to the Covered Man's face.

Like a striking cobra, the Covered Man grasped the doctor's wrist, making the doctor drop the pills. Kristine gasped.

"Hey! Be careful. Medicine is rare."

"No." The Covered Man tightened his grip around Doc Williamson's wrist. Not enough to break it but enough to make the woman wince in pain.

"I need to set your leg."

The Covered Man let go of the doctor's arm. "Do it."

Doc Williams glanced at Kristine again, now with a look of whether healing this person was worth the trouble.

"It's gonna hu—"

"Do. It."

Doc Williamson motioned for everyone but Joshua to hold him to the table.

She said to Joshua, "Follow my lead. We need to straighten the leg before setting it." As they held onto the Covered Man, Doc Williamson felt along the Covered Man's leg to locate the fracture. Once she was certain, she and Joshua pulled and twisted the leg to its original position.

Despite grabbing the cot so hard tight in both hands, the Covered Man did not flinch or make a sound.

Doc Williamson ran her hands along the leg to make certain that they set the bone right. Satisfied, the doctor grabbed the sections of wood and cloth from the floor and attached them to the Covered Man.

"Make sure he stays in bed for at least a week."

"How am I going to make sure someone who can toss cars around stays in bed?"

Doc Williamson shrugged. "He's your problem now." She packed up his gear and headed back outside with a stone-like appearance on her face.

"The doc was only trying to help you, you know." Kristine sat on the edge of the Covered Man's cot and smiled at him. "How can someone be so helpful and obnoxious at the same time?" She reached up toward his goggles.

The Covered Man sat up abruptly, causing Kristine to stand and step away.

"Don't."

"What is your problem? I just wanted to see you! You do so much for us. We don't know anything about you."

The Covered Man swung his good leg to the floor, his body tensing with pain as he tried to move his wounded leg to the floor as well.

Kristine tried to push him back to the cot. "H-Hey! The doc just told you not even five minutes ago you need to stay there for a week."

The Covered Man shoved her back, and using his good leg and arms, he pushed himself from the cot to a standing position. He wavered a bit as he got used to not putting weight on his wounded leg.

Kristine grappled with his arm to get him back into the cot. "Hey! Hey! You need to lie back down." The only reply was the Covered Man shaking her off and grasping his belt hanging over a nearby chair. Clasping it into place, he retrieved the sawed-off and his pistol and hung them on his belt. With a quick second make sure he had everything, he hobbled to the door.

As he emerged from The Shop, it took a moment for his eyes to adjust to the light, even with his goggles.

Joshua turned to look at him, then to Kristine, who stood behind him. "Doc just told me he is supposed to be laid up for a week."

Kristine looked at Joshua with a pleading gaze. "How the heck am I going to stop this guy?"

The Covered Man moved forward, toward his car. He saw at least a dozen new people. He wondered how long he was unconscious.

Joshua stepped in front of him and placed his hand on the Covered Man's chest. "Where do you think you're going? You're supposed to be resting."

"School. Is it far?"

"What? The old high school? Why would you go to that place?"

"Generators."

"You heard that, huh? Just put it out of your mind. What lives in that place sleeps now. But if you disturb it. We can all kiss our asses goodbye."

Joshua felt cold steel as the Covered Man placed the sawed-off against his nostrils.

"Move."

The world went quiet as all watched the two in the courtyard.

"What's your problem? You help us, then you turn on us?"

"The. Generators."

"Look for them elsewhere. What you're planning will be the end of you. And you will drag the rest of us into oblivion behind you."

"Dead settlement before. Dead settlement after."

Joshua gazed into the infinite black goggles of the man from the BeforeTimes. Then stepped aside.

The Covered Man put his sawed-off back into its holster, limped to his car and got in.

Joshua shouted, "Round up the young. We need to get anyone with kids to go back to where you came from."

"What?" Rays said. "We are abandoning Blac Arth? Some of the people just got here. They are exhausted from their travels."

"We can't take any chances. If *she* awakens, Blac Arth is dead."

Joshua said something else, but it couldn't be heard as the black car roared to life.

The citizens of Blac Arth did a great job fixing him, his vehicle, and parts of him he didn't even realize were broken. As he shifted the car into gear, Joshua moved to open the gate. He glanced at the Covered Man and shook his head in disappointment.

The Covered Man vowed to repay them the only way he knew how. The tires screeched as he tore out of the settlement and made it to 'the 14' and headed west.

STORY THREE

The Extent of Motherhood

Mike looked her in the eye and whispered, "I love you."
Susan blushed a little and smiled. "I love you too." She squeezed his hand a bit tighter.

The cacophony of noise of the high school hallway rushed over them like a wave. Students rushed down the hall and pushed past, some going to their lockers to deposit and retrieve books for their next class. Other students even going out to sneak a quick smoke before heading off to their next class.

"Hey, you two, get a room! Every time I see Mike, Susan is there." A taller boy in a letterman's jacket walked past and playfully bumped shoulders with Mike, almost forcing Mike's other hand to leave his pocket. "I am no longer sure if Susan is your shadow or if you are hers." He laughed obnoxiously at his own joke.

Mike shoved back and laughed. "Today more than ever, Steve. Today is our one-year anniversary!"

Steve looked at Susan. "One year? With this guy? Wow. You are a glutton for punishment."

Susan smiled and used her free hand to play with her long brown hair. "Steve! Mike is a great guy. He is always there and treats me well."

Steve grinned. "Well, you two lovies, I got to get to class." He slapped Mike on the shoulder and started walking down the hall but half spun around and looked at them both. "Catch the both of you later! Mike, don't forget about the game this weekend!"

"Wouldn't miss it!" He let go of Susan's hand to wave. Susan waved at Steve as well.

The warning bell rang, letting them know only a minute remained to get to their next designated spot.

Mike gasped, "My next class is soc! I have to hurry to make it." He trotted a few steps and turned back to Susan. "We still going out tonight?"

"Of course!" She blew a kiss and smiled, even though she did not mean it.

As she entered the classroom to find her seat, she thought back to how she and Mike met.

Mike was an avid member of Chess Club, and being that she was one of the top students of mathematics in school, their paths had crossed many times in school. She had known of him for a while, and he had this very "Boy next door" quality.

The day Mike saved the school after Brett Kelley started a fire in the chem lab really made him stand out. Mike, one of the most unobtrusive people in the whole school, saving people from the captain of the basketball team's chemistry mistake made many people see him in an exciting new light.

After that, many girls sought Mike's attention, even a few cheerleaders. But she knew him well since they roamed in the same social circles. Wherever Mike was, Susan tried to be as well. Her persistence paid off; eventually Mike did ask her out. She grinned to herself how nervous Mike was. Her pulse raced as she recalled the excitement of it. Her cheeks reddened a bit as the first time they were intimate bubbled up from her memory.

As the teacher began talking about the day's lesson, Susan's mind continued to drift, her hands taking notes but her mind wandering far away.

She had been with Mike for almost six months. Or was it nine? After the initial moment of excitement, Mike was mostly about routine. Sure he tried so hard to keep her happy, but that was the problem wasn't it? Tried so hard he became predictable. That is what drove her into the bed of his best friend a few months ago. She missed her period the last few months as well.

She sighed to herself as her mind drifted back to her schoolwork.

When the bell rang, she wandered through the mass exodus of students trying to escape the school on a Friday afternoon. She smiled at Mike when she met him at his car.

"Hey, Mike, can we go to Mazomanie, instead? I really do not want to face the crowds of Madison on a Friday night." She saw him stammer. The look on his face and the fact that he had to alter his plans made her smile internally. Anything to shake him out of his predictability, she thought.

"Sure."

She thought she saw a flash of regret on his face. But how could that be? Predictable as predictable can be.

As they pulled out of the parking lot, they began their small talk. Susan talked about the homework she had to do. Mike talked about some super on the East Coast capturing some villain. She wished he wouldn't pay so much attention to such things. That was a thousand miles away.

As they pulled out of the parking lot onto the main road, Susan was just nonchalantly agreeing with whatever Mike said while thinking about calling Steve later. She wanted to see him so badly. Yet, Steve was dating Michelle. She needed to find some way to win his heart while telling him about the missed periods.

"That is terrible," she said to Mike about whatever he was talking about. She hadn't even slept with Mike after the first two months of dating.

He was predictable in that area as well. So she knew it was Steve's child. If she could not drive a wedge between Steve and Michelle, she was sure Mike would step up and help her take care of the baby.

This thought snapped her out of her daydream.

Mike said, "We need to stop for gas before we get to Mazomanie. Luckily, I just got paid. It just jumped up to thirty-one-dollars a gallon."

Susan looked down at her belly and thought, Predicable but reliable.

"What the?" Mike said and began to slow down. There were police lights flashing ahead. In the long shadows of the waning afternoon, they could see what appeared to be a five-car pileup. It was where the road from the farming co-op exited onto the main road. A police car was stopped on their side of the pile up, its lights flashing but no siren.

"I wonder if that is Portia's dad?"

Susan said, "What?"

Mike said, "Portia's dad is a cop."

"Oh."

The collision blocked the road, so they slowed to a stop. They didn't see anyone.

Mike said, "Looks like some kind of accident."

"Well, duh."

Mike got out of the car and shouted, "Mr. White?"

The only reply was silence.

"Where is everyone?"

"I'm not sure if this police car belongs to Portia's father. Let me call Portia and have her check the car's numbers."

"Since when did you become an expert on the police?"

Mike just looked at her and shrugged.

Susan got all the way out of the car and added, "Maybe the ambulance has already taken everyone to the hospital?"

"And why would they just leave the cars in the middle of the road? In an hour it will be night; someone could slam into them."

Susan said, "Look at some of those cars. I wouldn't be caught dead driving them."

A slight tremor shook the ground.

"Whoa. An Earthquake," Susan said. "Didn't think we could get earthquakes in Wisconsin."

It seemed Mike didn't feel the quake or hear her. He walked over to the side of the road. She followed his gaze to some metallic object half hidden by the long grass.

"Sue, call 9-1-1."

"What? I am sure they already…"

"Just do it!" He reached down and picked up a pistol. It looked brand new.

Susan pulled out her phone.

Mike popped the clip. No bullets fired. He replaced the clip and tucked the gun into his belt against his back. Susan wondered where he learned to handle a weapon. A few months ago he would turn pale at the sight of blood.

"Hello? Yes, we are out on Highway 14, out by the old co-op and there is some kind of accident here."

Mike continued to look around the area. Maybe the officer was struck by a car and lying in the tall grass. Then where are all the owners for the vehicles? Maybe they were afraid after striking a police officer and they fled? And one driver somehow caused a five-car pileup? Or all five drivers struck a police officer and all fled? None of these stories made sense.

Susan continued, "There about five cars in an accident, blocking most of the road. Yeah. Right where the entrance to the co-op meets the highway."

Mike took two steps into the tall grass when he saw numerous holes in the ground. He could only see two, no, three, mostly hidden by the tall grass. Each was about two feet in diameter. Could the missing people have fallen down these holes? If one fell, why would the rest not see the holes and avoid them? More questions with no answers.

Susan moved the phone to her other ear. "There is a police car also. But no sign of anyone. We found a gun on the side of the road. It looks new. Yeah."

Mike peered into one of the holes. The walls were smooth, as if it was professionally dug, like for a well or something. Another small tremor shook the ground and he almost lost his balance. He didn't think he would fall in, but he didn't want to take any chances either. This whole thing made him easy. He heard something clank and scrape from the car pileup behind him.

Susan continued, "Yeah, you really can't miss it. Okay. The lights? We can stay for ten minutes. Really?" She sighed heavily. "We cannot stay all night. People might get hurt." She hung up her phone and put it in her pocket. "Hey Mike! No one is coming. They just want us to turn on our warning lights to make sure people can see us, y'know, cuz it's getting late." She saw Mike walking closer to the car pileup. "Did you hear me? No one is coming. We need to get out of here."

Mike crept closer to a wrecked truck. It slammed so hard into one of the other cars, it was actually sitting a short way off of the road, resting on the trunk of the car it hit.

He heard something scraping on the road underneath the truck. He crouched down, his hand slowly going for the gun at his back.

Underneath the car was Principal Schwab. Her eyes were crazed with fear and rolled back to the back of her head with shock. It was then Mike saw her left leg ended at the knee. Blood seeped out onto the ground.

Another tremor, this time it felt like it was directly beneath his feet.

"It's Principal Schwab!" he said. "It looks like she's hurt!"

Susan started to run forward, but Mike yelled, "Don't come any closer! There is something wrong with her!"

Susan bit her lower lip and put her hands on her hips. "You failed first aid, you dunce. I can—"

"Susan. Something is wrong here! Just turn on those lights!"

Susan clamped her mouth shut. When did he become so bossy? Maybe she misjudged Mike. She thought about what to tell him about the missed periods, completely ignoring the car's hazard lights.

"Mrs. Schwab? Can you hear me? I am going to pull you out of there. Help is on the way."

A tremor shook the ground so hard it felt as if a bomb went off. It sent both Susan and Mike to their hands and knees.

The road began to crack underneath them.

"Mike, we need to get out of here!"

Large chunks of asphalt began to crumble inward. Mrs. Schwab disappeared from view as she, the truck and one of the nearby cars all fell inward, into the hole.

"Oh my God!"

The hole began to widen. Cracks appeared in the road like a strange macabre dance of lines.

"Mrs. Schwab!" Mike yelled.

Another tremor hit, jostling them both so hard they both almost fell to the ground...

Suddenly, Susan felt her survival instinct kick in. She would do anything to save the unborn life inside of her. "Mike, we need to go!" She started running to the car.

Mike looked from her to the expanding hole as another car slid into it. He took off after Susan.

Susan reached the car. She turned around and saw Mike two steps behind her. She got in the passenger side, and by the time she slammed her door shut, Mike had the key in the ignition and the engine came to life.

Throwing it into reverse, the tires squealed, and the fourth car teetered on the brink of the hole. Mike spun the car around and pushed his foot to the floor, speeding back in the direction of the school.

Mike said, "What the heck just happened?"

Susan said, "A sinkhole?"

Mike said, "I never heard of sink holes around here."

"Then what was that?! Principal Schwab is dead! Oh my God. Oh my God!"

"We don't know that; she could…"

"She fell into a hole and cars fell in after her! Oh my God. What is going on?"

They peeled into the school parking lot. Most of the students and faculties cars were gone for the weekend. But they had to try and get help somewhere.

He drove up right by the school where a group of students stood talking. It looked like some of the football team, including the star quarterback, Todd. He drove up so fast they scattered, even though they stood on the curb.

As he slammed on the brakes, some of them shouted at him, "What the fuck are you doing?" Another said, "Where did you get your license?"

"Hey, that's Susan and Mike? Didn't they leave already?"

Mike got out of the car. He looked pale and was damp with sweat. "Hey! We need help!"

"Yeah, you need to retake drivers ed, obviously"

"Shut up, Todd! This is serious!"

A few of them opened their mouth to protest, but as Susan got out of the car and they saw how they both appeared scared to death, they began to question what was happening.

Susan walked up to Mike. "Mike's right. There was some kind of accident up the road. She stammered as if her mouth wouldn't work. "Principal Schwab is dead."

There were a few gasps, but Jay let out a "Woohoo!"

Mike looked at him with cold steel in his eyes. "This is no joke, asshole. She's dead. There was some kind of accident up the road by the co-op."

"Do you think rioters attacked the co-op? I heard there were food riots in South Madison last week."

He swallowed and looked at Susan. "There was some kind of quake..."

Betty said, "Yeah. What is that? I thought we never get earthquakes in the Midwest, but there must have been three in the last hour." She looked around at the others who agreed.

"An odd occurrence." Everyone turned and saw Ms. Ghariani, the vice principal, heading out of the school toward them. "But I am sure there is a logical reason. Please put out whatever you are smoking, Mister Johnson. You are still on school grounds."

Mister Hemm, the English teacher, followed her, and Tim, the leader of chess club. Jay threw the hand-rolled cigarette on the ground and crushed it with his shoe.

Mike ran up to Tim and grasped his upper arms tightly, "Tim. Tim. You have to tell me, is Portia still here?"

Before any answer could be spoken, Ms. Ghariani interrupted, "School is closing people. If you do not have extracurricular activities," her voice was stern but she kept a polite smile on her lips,

"I am sure you can find more pleasant things to do on a Friday evening than hang out in front of school?"

When Susan spoke, her voice wavered. "Ms. Ghariani. The principal was killed, just up the road from here."

"What?"

"Honest. There was some kind of accident…"

Ms. Ghariani regained her composure quickly and interrupted, but her voice still wavered. "Did you call 9-1-1?"

"Yes. But they just gave me the run around about being understaffed."

The vice principal stood for a moment. If she had any inner emotions, she concealed them well.

"Mike. Sue," she said. "Let's go back inside and try to call again. Everyone else should head home."

Todd spoke up. "You kidding? It's not every Friday coach cancels practice! We are heading out to paaaaartay!" After meeting Ms. Ghariani's gaze, he caught what he was saying in his throat and lowered his voice. "Uh, within reason, of course."

Mike asked, "Practice was canceled? Why?" Usually the only people in school on Friday night were football players and the students in chess club. Maybe a few stragglers in the library or band members practicing.

Todd said, "Yeah. We were changing in the locker room and we felt one of those quakes."

Jay added, "Yeah, Janitor George told coach there was some kind of giant hole where the field used to be.

Susan and Mike gave each other a panicked look. Susan asked, "Jay, are you sure?"

We all went out to look. Sure as shi –" He coughed and looked at Ms. Ghariani's stern gaze. "Sure as stuff, a huge hole. Right in the middle of the field. George and coach should still be out there."

Tim interrupted. "Technically a sinkhole is usually formed when water moves soil into some underground void like a cave or cavern. The overlying soil and subsoil then collapse creating what we call a sinkhole at the surface level. In the upper Midwest, sinkholes are common yet rarely exceed five feet in diameter and twenty feet deep. It is quite possible that it could be the beginnings of a karst that…"

"Shut up, Tim!"

A police siren was heard coming from the south. They all sat and stared as the police car eventually raced by going north. Another quake shook the ground. The sirens stopped abruptly and something that sounded like gunshots or fireworks were heard.

Mister Hemm looked at Ms. Ghariani. "I will go check the football field." He turned and walked at a brisk pace back into the building.

Mike looked at Tim like he was just shaken awake and asked again, "Tim, is Portia still here?"

"She should be, I just left chess club since no one could beat me, as usual. I was just following our beloved vice principal, here, to see if we could conduct a bake sale to maybe procure a better room for our activities instead of down by the music room. During the week when they have practice, the noise is quite…"

Another quake shook the ground, this time with such force it almost sent them to the ground. When the tremor stopped, Jay said, "Fuck this, let's get out of here!" He and the rest of the football players, except Todd, made a break for their cars.

Todd, who still stood in front of the school, yelled after them, "Wait, come back! We don't know what's going on!"

None of them listened as they raced toward their cars.

Tyler made it to his car first and peeled out, racing toward the highway. Jay followed close behind.

As Tyler made it to the highway, another quake struck. The section of road connecting the school to the highway collapsed, swallowing Jay's car.

"Holy Shit!" people cried.

Tyler swerved his car heavily to the left, missing the widening hole. He pushed the gas pedal to the floor to try and make it to the other exit. As he made the final turn onto the highway, another shock struck. The ground shook so hard, all of them were thrown to the ground.

When they finally were able to stand back up, both exits to the highway were collapsed, along with a third of the parking lot. If this had happened during school hours, at least thirty cars would have been swallowed.

Todd spoke first. "Oh my God! Jay!" He stood up and ran to the edge of the hole.

Mike shouted after him, "Stop! Wait! You don't know what's down there!"

Tim stood up and ran after Todd. "C'mon, Mike! We got to see this! A geological disturbance like this is a once in a lifetime thing!"

Betty struggled to her feet. "Those two are nuts."

Ms. Ghariani stood as well and shouted, "You two get back here! We don't know if that's safe!"

Todd stopped and turned, allowing a much slower Tim to catch up and pass him. Todd shouted back, "That is exactly why we need to look! Jay could be hurt or worse! Once we check, we will come back. We won't try to move him or nothin', just to see if he is okay!" With that he spun back and chased after the heavily wheezing Tim.

Ms. Ghariani pursed her lips in disappointment, then pulled out her phone and dialed 9-1-1.

Susan watched as Tim and Todd reached the edge of the hole. Tim knelt down to inspect something at the side of the hole but at a distance Susan could not see what it was. She heard Todd yell, "Jay! Jay can you hear me!"

Ms. Gharinani said, "Hello. Yes. Yes. We have an emergency. We are at the Heights High School. This is Mina Ghariani, the vice principal. We have quite the emergency here. Half of our parking lot has collapsed. I know. I know about that but this is an emergency. Some of the students were swallowed up by the hole, vehicles and all! What do you mean there is no one? Can you at least send an ambulance? These student's lives might be in jeopardy!"

The ground trembled once again. Susan saw something that looked like a telephone pole with purple striations shoot up into the sky. It swayed for a moment, like a cobra listening to a flute, then came down on Tim and snatched him up with what appeared to be its mouth.

Tim screamed for help, a disturbing cry that shook them to their bones. They watched in shock as he disappeared from view inside of it.

By the time the shock wore off, Todd started running back toward the school. Ms. Ghariani was frantically screaming into the phone. "Oh my God! It just ate one of my students, do you hear! It ate him!"

Mike was shouting for Todd to run faster.

The pole-like object that just devoured Tim dropped to the ground and pushed its way forward. Susan's panic-stricken mind could not comprehend much but still thought it looked like some monstrous earthworm the way it propelled itself on the ground.

As they saw the thing crawl toward them, they all ran inside to the school. Ms. Ghariani handed her phone to Susan and took a ring of keys from her purse. She locked the doors. The worm-thing slammed into the glass in the door, and a spider-web-like crack appeared where it struck.

She quickly locked the other door. Then moving to the inner sets of doors, she promptly locked those as well.

The worm-thing bumped up against the doors, a bit lighter this time. Close up, it did look similar to a monstrous earthworm. It pressed itself against the glass a few more times. Then realizing it could not get through this substance, it swayed its head back and forth a bit, then moved to a section of lawn next to the concrete sidewalk and began to burrow into it. It must have been at least thirty to forty feet long and two or three feet in diameter.

Susan handed the phone back to Ms. Ghariani. "I think they hung up."

"I don't blame them."

Todd panted heavily, bent over, his hands on his knees.

"Jay. Jesus. Can't believe it. Jay."

Betty rubbed his back in an attempt to comfort him. "What did we just see? What is happening? Can't we call the police?"

Ms. Ghariani said, "I did. They said they are understaffed…" She looked at Susan. "Just like you told me."

"Then what are we going to do?" Betty asked.

Right now, we need to round up who we can and bring them to the gym. We use that room in case of tornadoes; should be strong enough to withstand… whatever is going on until help comes.

"But what if it's not?"

"Don't think like that. Tell people to go there."

"Portia!" Mike ran off.

Ms. Ghariani shouted after him, "Mike! Don't go alone!"

"I'll go with him!" Susan said as she took off after him. "Mike! Mike, wait up!"

Mike raced through the hallways, occasionally seeing a student yet rushing past, not saying a thing.

Susan shouted at them as she ran, "Ms. Ghariani said everyone needs to meet in the gymnasium!"

Mike headed to the underground level of classrooms. The kids called the area "The Dungeon" since the rooms here were half underground. They were rooms where things like band practice and extra circular activities were held. He sprinted down the hall, Susan a few steps behind him.

They passed the doors to the custodian rooms where the furnaces were located along with all the janitorial equipment. He reached an intersection and took a sharp turn to the right. They came to a door with a sheet of paper taped to it that had "CHESS CLUB" written on it with black marker.

Mike tore open the door. There were a few people inside, preoccupied with their chessboards. The president of the club, a senior named Gerald, was playing against Portia. He studied the board intently as they entered but looked up at Mike as he approached.

"Hey, Mike. We already started this round but we can get you into the next one."

Mike ignored him and pulled Portia to her feet and hugged her. "Thank goodness you are all right."

Portia looked happy to see him but glanced at Susan. "Mike. What are you doing here? I thought…"

"We ran across some trouble up at the old co-op. There are these worms. We saw your father's patrol car. Half the football team tried to escape…We're trapped here."

The other chess players looked up from their games and looked at Mike. One of them whispered, "Shhh!" before going back to studying his board.

Gerald said, "What? What do worms have to do with the police?"

Mike grabbed Portia by the hand.

"We need to get out of here!"

Portia tore her hand from Mike's grasp. "Are you kidding? I am playing the best game in my life! No way Gerald is going to win today!"

Gerald grinned. "Oh, you think so, huh?"

"Portia! Please!" Mike reached into his belt and pulled out the pistol.

Portia stared in disbelief. "Is that…dad's pistol?"

"I am pretty sure it is. I found it next to his abandoned squad car."

The floor began to shake.

Mike grabbed Portia's hand. "We need to go. Now!"

As Mike pulled Portia to the doorway, the floor erupted in shards of broken cement block and dirt. A brownish worm with purple striations through its body burst through the floor. The worm snapped up the two chess players at the far side of the room and they were gone.

"Oh my God!" Gerald shouted as the floor continued to shake.

Mike pulled Portia after him as he raced out into the hallway. Susan and Gerald followed behind. Another worm burst through the floor, cutting off the escape for the rest of the chess players.

Gerald managed a last scream before one of the worms clamped down on his head.

As Mike turned left to head back to where they entered the Dungeon, a worm burst through the concrete wall. It appeared about halfway between where they stood and the stairs back to the ground floor. They had to find another way out.

The only other stairway Mike knew of was at the other end of the band room practice hall. He headed right to try and make it there before the worms blocked that off as well. They ran past a few hallways, some of them had students emerging from them with looks of bewilderment on their faces. All they could do was shout, "Run!" as they flew past, not daring to stop and explain.

They passed the band room and took a ninety degree turn to the stairway and stopped in their tracks. The staircase had collapsed. Looking back down the hall they just came from, they saw one of the worms heading toward them, snapping up students unlucky enough to not get out of its way.

Portia said, "What are we going to do?"

Susan said, "Into the band room!" She grabbed Mike's hand and yanked him so hard he lost his grasp with Portia.

As they entered the band room, they saw the hole in the floor and ceiling. Susan pulled Mike over to the debris hanging from the ceiling and shouted, "Climb!"

"What?"

"It's our only way out!"

Mike helped Susan hold onto a beam, and she struggled to get decent handholds to shimmy up the debris. Mike then helped Portia up next.

"Gym was never my strong suite," she said.

"Come on Portia!" He jumped as high as he could and grabbed onto other broken beams and metal rods that once held the ceiling tiles and fluorescent lights in place. The jagged edges of the torn metal cut into his hands. He felt a surge of adrenaline as he saw Susan reach the lip of the floor above and drag herself onto it.

He looked back down at Portia, who was only about two hand widths behind him. Her eyes wide with fear and strain.

As Mike grabbed the lip to pull himself onto the next floor, he heard both of the girls shriek.

"Climb! Mike! Climb!"

"Hurry!"

As Mike got an arm over the lip, he dared a glance below him. He saw Portia struggling as hard as she could, the sweat beading on her brow. Emerging from the darkness below was the largest worm they saw yet. As its maw opened, it had almost a human quality to it. It even had vaguely human-like looking teeth.

Mike yelled at the top of his lungs, "Climb, Portia! Climb!"

Mike pulled himself up, over the edge. He spun himself around and extended his right hand down to grasp Portia's.

"Hurry!" he shouted as he stretched his hand out as far as he could. He felt her fingertips brush his, and extending himself with his toes, he grasped Portia's hand firmly.

"I got you!"

It was then the Worm grabbed Portia with its odd maw, its momentum carrying them all upward and lifting Mike up off the floor.

"Mike! Let go!"

Mike screamed back, "I can't! Not without her!"

The worm began to slurp Portia into its gullet, Portia gripping Mike's hand in terror.

"Mike! "Let go!"

Mike's hand touched the lips of the Maw Worm. They were soft and coasted with a thin slime, like picking up an earthworm after a long summer rain. It curled its lips to allow him to be dragged along with Portia.

Portia screamed, "It burns! I can't feel my legs! Help me, Mike! Help me!"

Mike kicked his foot up and placed it next to the maw of the worm and with all of his might pushed out with his leg to wrench himself from Portia's grasp. As he slammed into the floor, the wind was knocked out of him. Susan dragged him to his feet. They saw the lump in the worm's throat slowly move down to its gullet.

"Portiaaaaa!" Mike shouted.

"Let's get out of here!" Susan said, and she clasped Mike's hand.

As they ran toward the gymnasium, Susan glanced over her shoulder. "This one isn't following."

Mike followed her gaze. The Worm stood almost cobra-like as if it was studying them. Watching them with an eyeless face.

"Who cares? Run!"

They made it to the gymnasium. The main lights were out and only the backup generator lights still worked, giving the area a thick gloom. Mr. Hemm was also there pacing back and forth with his phone to his ear. Ms. Ghariani was trying to dial someone on her phone as well. Todd and Betty sat on the bleachers, arms wrapped around each other. These must be all the surviving students in the building, all of them still had a look of bewilderment on their faces.

Ms. Ghariani saw them and strode over to them, trying to appear strong, "What's wrong?"

Susan wheezed as she tried to catcher her breath. "Another worm. Bigger than the rest. Got Portia."

"Did anyone else make it from The Dungeon?" When Susan and Mike shook their heads, she slumped a bit, her expression turning dour.

"What are we going to do?" said Susan.

"I don't know, Susan. I don't know."

Susan sneered at him, her emotion switching from shock to anger. "But you sure know a lot about Portia, don't you? You grabbed her hand instead of mine!"

"I cannot believe you are bringing this up now. She was just killed!"

Susan opened her mouth to shout something but then closed it. Everyone sat in shock and stared at each other.

Mr. Hemm clicked his phone off in disgust. "I truly cannot believe it. 9-1-1 said it would at least be an hour before help gets here, maybe two. They are short staffed."

Ms. Ghariani looked at the phone and said, "That is what they told me when we were in front of the building as well."

The ground shook as they felt something slam into the floor. Betty shrieked and buried her face into Todd's shoulder. Those who were standing grabbed onto something or someone to steady themselves.

"Do…do you think they can bust into here?"

Ms. Ghariani shook her head. "I don't know. The gym is designed to withstand tornadoes, but this."

The floor shook again, and a crack formed in the floor.

Ms. Ghariani shouted, "We need to go!"

Todd replied, "Go where?"

Ms. Ghariani said, "They'll get us if we stay!"

Betty said, "If we leave, they'll be on us before we get outside!"

Mr. Hemm said, "We can't just wait here!"

To punctuate the thought, the floor shook again. Another crack danced along the floor, widening as it went. Everyone backed away, looking around in a panic for someone to come up with a plan.

Ms. Ghariani said, "I think we are going to have to make a break for it."

Mr. Hemm grabbed three metal poles used for pulling out the bleachers. He tossed one to Todd and one to Mike. "The exits to the outside here lead to the football field, not to mention they lead in an opposite direction of the parking lot."

Todd added, "Plus, it's collapsed. The entire thing is one big hole."

Mr. Hemm nodded and continued, "So the front doors are the way to go to get head back to Black Earth. If we can at least make it back to the gas station, we can hopefully convince someone to come help us." None of them looked confident with this plan.

A section of floor heaved upward as the floor shook again. "Let's go!" Ms. Ghariani shouted.

The small group ran forward down the hall, toward the nearest glass door exit. The flickering of the lights overhead contrasted with the darkness of freedom outside.

They made it about halfway to the door when the floor collapsed. With a roar of crumbling concrete and smashing beams, they tumbled into the hallway beneath them.

Before they could regain their feet, a worm struck and grabbed Ms. Ghariani.

Mr. Hemm dropped his pole and leapt up to grasp the ledge above him and pull himself up.

Ms. Ghariani screamed with an outstretched arm, "John!"

Whether he heard or not, he ran out of sight.

As those who remained attempted to scramble away, the worm pulled Ms. Ghariani into its throat, like a sock devouring a foot.

As the worm reeled back to gulp down its meal, the floor next to it erupted. The massive bulk of the Maw Worm emerged. With its strange human-like mouth, it clamped down on the other worm, startling it so much, it coughed up Ms. Ghariani.

She struck the floor of the half-collapsed hallway. Her flesh sizzled from the corrosive digestive juices she was soaking in just a moment before.

Parts of her skull were exposed to the air, and her feet were completely dissolved. She gurgled a scream through her half-digested face. Her one working arm flailed wildly.

The shriek from Betty was long and shrill. Her body shook and a bit of bile crept up into her throat, giving the scream a slight gurgling sound. Her legs visibly shook, and it appeared that they would give out entirely. Todd stood rooted to the ground for a moment, his mind not firmly grasping what exactly was happening.

As the last of the worm disappeared into the Maw Worm, it looked up at Todd and a voice echoed into everyone's minds. "Todd. Don't run." It was Jay's voice. All of them stopped in their tracks.

"You look so tired buddy. Why don't you rest for a bit?"

"Jay? Where did you come from?" Both Todd and Betty took a step toward the Maw Worm.

Mike grabbed Todd's shoulder. "C'mon, man, let's get out of here!"

"But Jay's here! Maybe he needs medical attention!"

Mike said, "Jay? What?" Todd's gaze was fixated on the worm. Mike could feel that it somehow was staring at them.

Susan's voice trembled as she said, "Let's go! That's not Jay!"

Betty appeared to snap awake, like she was just woken from a deep sleep. She looked around confused.

Todd walked forward again.

Betty blinked and shook her head. "Todd!"

Todd heard Jay's voice in his head again. "Todd. You remember how we were friends since we were young. We used to go down by the steam and fish every summer. When your car broke down last year, I helped you fix it."

As Todd walked forward, the worm opened its mouth from floor to ceiling, a living tunnel, ready to swallow Todd whole as he strode, zombie-like, toward it.

"Todd!" Betty shouted and ran to his side. She pulled on his arm. "Run! We need to get away from that thing!" As she began to pull him away, he had the same bewildered look on his face that she did just a moment ago.

"Betty? Betty Where's Jay? I heard him."

Betty wiped away the tears and grime that smudged her cheek. "Honey, we need to get out of here…"

With one quick snap, Todd was gone. The force of the Maw Worm lunging forward to devour him, knocked Betty back a few feet. "Nooooo!"

Mike shouted, "Betty, run!" Susan grabbed her arm, and they turned to flee down the dimly lit corridor of the half-collapsed remains of The Dungeon.

The worm just stared after them as they ran.

"Betty! Come join me!" It was Todd's voice.

"T-Todd. Todd, where are you?"

"In a place free of pain, or wants. No need to struggle anymore."

Betty fell to her knees. "Todd. That can't be you."

"Betty. Can't you hear me? Of course it's me. Haven't I been loyal to you in the three years we have been together?"

"Yes. But. I saw you…" She pressed her fingers against her eyes and dug harder into her optic globes. The clear liquid in her eye sockets began to dribble down her face. "Todd! I saw you!"

Mike and Susan slowly backed away from Betty as the Maw Worm edged closer. Instead of looking down at its prey, it faced Mike and Susan.

"How could you be with her, Mikey? You know I love you more." It was Portia's voice.

Mike opened his mouth to say something, but Susan yanked his arm hard. Mike looked at her, snapping him back to reality. They both turned and bolted. Fleeing headlong into the dimly lit corridors.

They approached the stairway they came down earlier when they were looking for Portia. However, it had now collapsed. Broken beams and metal sheets that used to belong to the floor above had completely blocked off any chance of escape.

Susan shouted, "Maybe the band room is still accessible!"

They ran down the hall, only to run into a collapsed ceiling around the hallway they first saw the Maw dine on another worm.

With panic and disappointment in her voice, Susan said "Now what?"

Mike looked around. The door to the custodian's room was nearby, and the door was slightly open.

"Susan! Here!" Mike kicked the door open and ran inside. Susan following after. The custodian's room was in shambles. Brooms, mops and tools lay strewn across the floor, most likely because of the earthquakes.

After Susan ran through the door, Mike took the pipe he held and jammed it through the handles of the door to hold it in place.

"You really think a barred door will slow down something that can burrow through the floor?"

Susan saw another door at the back of the room and ran toward it.

"We have to do something!" Mike said as he ran after her.

A wall of hot, dry air struck them in the face as they entered the boiler room. Four large boilers sat in the area, two on each of the side walls. Ahead lie more discarded tools scattered everywhere and a door to a small storage closet sat open along the back of the room. Two gas-powered generators sat in the corner of the closet, next to the door.

Susan asked in a whisper, "What are we going to do?"

Mike replied in the same hushed tone, "What can we do? Lie low here for maybe ten or twenty minutes, then see if we can make a break for it."

"That thing will get us!"

"I am pretty sure Mr. Hemm got away. If he made it, so can we."

As the adrenaline wore off, the shock of what happened began to weigh heavily on them. Susan choked back tears and said, "Betty. Todd. So many of our friends. Gone."

Mike choked out, "Yeah."

"What are those things, Mike?"

Mike kept staring at his feet. "Giant worms? Jeez, I don't know."

Susan put her face in her hands. "I just want to go home. I just want things back the way they were."

Mike glanced up and looked at her.

"I remember when I first met you in middle school," Susan said. "You were doodling race cars in your notebook."

"They weren't race cars; it was the Batmobile, and he was chasing the Joker."

"The point is, we didn't know about what the world really was. The riots. The lootings. Not being able to buy meat every day. Tech companies overthrowing the government. The mega AI that watches our every move. Sections of the coastline going underwater. We just lived, hoping that the summer never ended."

"What's your point?"

"We should have seen this coming."

"Susan. How could anyone know these things would appear?"

"Not these things specifically, but haven't you felt that things were slipping away from us? That civilization was swirling the drain?"

"I don't think monsters appearing have anything to do with..."

"Maybe with the decline of human civilization, it was just a matter of time before something stepped up to take our place."

"So giant worms just evolved over night to take our place?"

"Not overnight. Maybe they grew somewhere?"

"You are so full of shit."

Susan's despair burned into anger, and she hit Mike on the arm, "You asshole. Don't say I'm full of shit. You think I don't know about your feelings for Portia?"

"Yeah. Because I am dating her."

"What?" Susan's jaw dropped, "Then what about our date? Before everything fell apart we were going on a date tonight!"

The ground shook a bit.

"I wanted to buy you dinner one last time. After dinner I was planning on breaking up with you." He shrugged. "I thought it was kind of a courtesy."

"I don't believe you! You were cheating on me? You fucker! I am pregnant with your child!"

"It's not my child, Susan, and you know it."

Tears welled up in her eyes. "How can you say that to me? You know this is your child!"

"Not according to Steve."

"Wh-what?"

"You heard me. Shortly after you slept with him, he came up to me and bragged about sleeping with you. Haven't you noticed we haven't fooled around in a few months? Didn't you wonder why?"

Susan just stared with her mouth open, trying to scream or cry or anything, but no sound came out.

"We didn't have sex for a few weeks. After he told me that, I was stunned. At first I didn't care; I was planning on loving you just the same. But Portia asked me what was on my mind, and one thing led to another. She was kind and supportive."

"How could you do this to me, Mike?"

"You didn't care about what you did to me. How can I trust you again?"

"But I love you!"

"Would you trust me again if the roles were reversed?"

Susan opened her mouth, but her voice only cracked.

"Mike." Portia's voice echoed in their minds.

Mike stared at his feet again. "Portia. You were so good to me. I miss you already."

"We can be together again, Mike."

The center of the floor cracked and began to crumble away.

Mike buried his face in his hands. "I even miss your dad. That weekend we went camping was one of the best times in my life."

"You went camping with Portia? And her dad? When did you do this?"

The hole in the center of the floor grew wider as the floor trembled and collapsed a bit more.

"Mike. We had a great time with you as well." The voice was Portia's dad. "Once you join us, we can go camping again. We will all be together again."

Susan grabbed Mike's shoulders. "Mike. Mike. Snap out of it!"

As the hole widened even farther, Mike got to his feet. He stared down into the hole and saw the Maw Worm waiting, its human-like mouth wide open.

"Mike. Mike what are you doing?"

"I'm tired, Sue. I found true happiness. Someone who made me happier than ever before. The way the world is. As everything slowly falls apart. That one ray of light I had was taken from me. But I can be united again."

"No! No! Snap out of it! That thing is affecting your mind somehow. Can't you see that?"

Mike took a step forward so he stood on the edge of the pit.

"No!" Susan screamed as she pulled the gun from Mike's belt and fired into the hole twice. The recoil propelled her backwards, causing her to almost trip and fall. If the bullets had any effect, the Maw Worm didn't show it.

Mike looked over at her with a sad expression, and then jumped feet first into the hole.

"Miiiike!" Susan screamed as she regained her footing.

"Mike!" She screamed again. She ran to the edge of the hole with hope against hope she would still see Mike there, hanging onto a random outcropping of rock. Instead, she was greeted with the Maw Worm, slowly rising up to meet her. No sign of Mike.

Susan quickly backed away from the hole. Terrified to run past it, she ran inside the storage closet and shut the door. She picked up a discarded hammer and wedged it behind the handle, keeping the door from opening.

Holding the pistol out in front of her, she scrambled backwards, crab-like, to the far back corner of the closet. Her breaths came in little gasps as she tried to hold back the tears and despair. A few moments went by. The only sounds she heard being her own heartbeat.

Her voice cracked as she said, "Leave me alone. I just want to have my baby."

"Susan." A voice came from directly on the other side of the door. It was Mike.

"Susan." Mike said again, "No need to fear. Why don't you come out and join us? Todd is here, and Betty. All of your friends."

As quiet as a mouse Susan said, "Leave me alone. Please leave me alone."

Mike said, "Guess who else is here with us? You will never believe it."

"Hey! How's my girl? And my son! I can hope it's a son, can't I?"

"Steve?"

"Yeah, my darlin' girl. I'm here. Open the door so we can be a family again."

"No! It's not real! You are that thing! That damnable worm! Those voices aren't real! You are not them!"

Susan then saw a shimmer pass through the door and through her. It looked like a ripple on a calm lake, but only in the air.

A voice spoke again, but this time it was not a voice of someone she knew, it was inhuman, liquidy, muted and garbled, as if someone was talking underwater. A faint female quality was part of it, but that was the only part that resembled a human voice.

"We are them. Since they all lie within. Slowly being devoured. I can feel their flesh dissolve in my stomach. Worm and human alike. But don't worry, sweet Susan. My darlin' girl. You will soon be a family again."

The door bent inward as if something heavy was being pressed or pushed against it, but then it slowly snapped back into shape. It pushed inward again, this time the hinges of the door creaked and groaned under the strain. Susan held the pistol out in front of her, muzzle pointed at the door.

"Please stop. Please. Please stop."

The strain on the door resumed once again, but the door now sat slightly off center from the broken hinges.

Susan placed the barrel of the pistol against her chin.

As the door began to buckle inward a third time, she put her free hand on her stomach, looked down and said, "I love you." She closed her eyes, and the explosion of the pistol rang in her ears.

STORY FOUR

Into the Maw

The black car drove up 'the 14', slowing to a crawl in front of a high school, now laying in ruins. The driveway into the main parking lot crumbled away into a hole about twenty feet in diameter. After the car's engine rumbled to a stop, the Covered Man got out. He limped over to the edge of the hole. Peering in, he saw a car half covered in dirt.

The car had been there for years, he surmised, probably after the time of the actual Collapse. The back end of it stuck up from the bottom of the half collapsed hole. Dirt was sprinkled across it as the sides began to cave in, most likely from the years and the weather.

Surveying the area, he looked for a way to get his car into the parking lot. He gauged the distance of having to carry two generators this far in his wounded state to building some sort of bridge. Thinking back to the reaction of the Blac Arthers to this place, he opted for getting his vehicle as close as possible.

The ditch alongside the road was too steep and he risked bottoming out his vehicle if he went that route. The other exit of the parking lot seems to have a similar collapse to this one.

There were older rusty vehicles in the parking lot; most had given in to age. He did see one car that had three flat tires but that would suit his purpose nicely.

Hobbling over to the abandoned car, he put his back against the trunk. The muscles in his good leg knotted as he moved it a few feet from its ancient resting place. The asphalt underneath was a deeper black. Minutes passed by as he moved the car to the wide hole.

He wiped his brow despite the fact his suit whisked any perspiration away, an involuntary reaction from ages gone by. The Covered Man flipped the car onto its side and spun it ninety degrees. Despite his injuries he flexed his muscles and with a final heave, he rolled the car into the hole, rolling it so the undercarriage faced upward. He leapt into the hole to dig around the edges of the car to make sure the bottom of it was flush with the earth around it.

He felt a tremor. The earth continued to shake for a moment, as if something awoke after years of being asleep.

The Covered Man's hand instantly went to the sawed-off on his belt. He looked about as a minute ticked by, then another. When nothing appeared, he finished his work then placed his hand on the side of the overturned car to help pull himself out of the hole. Pain shot up his leg as he pushed off the car. He tried to ignore it since he knew whatever the Blac Arthers feared, dwelled somewhere within.

He opened the door of the black car and had to physically grab his wounded leg and lift it into the car. He sat for a moment and stared at the ceiling, waiting for the pain to subside.

The car stirred to life once again, and with the driver's door open a bit so he could look down at his tries and make certain he stayed on the narrow makeshift bridge. It inched forward, shifting once it hit the unevenness of his makeshift bridge. It bumped and heaved and almost got stuck, but revving the engine and applying the gas got him into the school's parking lot.

Pulling up to the school entrance, he again had to lift his leg to get it out. Getting out of that crater hurt his already wounded leg more than he thought. He hoped it would hold out long enough to get the generators, if they even still existed.

By the state of this building he guessed they most likely did. The building had been almost completely overgrown by vines and creepers. Over the years the plants had pulled down sections of the structure. Piles of brick lie along the building's base.

The Covered Man limped up to the doorway to enter the school. The doors that were once there, were missing. Some of the creepers have begun to extend their fingers into the building's interior.

As he entered, everything was shrouded in gloom. Luckily, enough light came in from between the vines that the Covered Man did not have to use any special means to see where he was going.

The entry hall had offices to the left and right. Directly ahead the corridor continued, with a diagonal branch to the left. The floor in that area had a huge hole in it. For an abandoned building, he found it devoid of the typical graffiti that usually caked the walls.

A voice came from the offices to his left. "Why are you here?"

The Covered Man turned to look in the direction of the voice. It was one of the Broken: those who were subjugated to genetic experiments and had their DNA pulled apart like taffy, then put back together.

He looked like a raider on hard times. One of his boots was missing. The pants and shoe he worn were in tatters and heavily stained. His dark hair was in patches. Parts of his scalp were bald, yet where he did have hair, it drooped to his shoulders. His beard was in the same spotty, shaggy state. Standing near the entrance to the outside, the man blinked heavily from the sunlight that streamed in. The degenerate form wielded a heavy wrench. He tightened his grip on it.

"Passing through." The Covered Man heard the soft shuffle behind him, about where the door was to the other set of offices.

"Mother doesn't want you here." The corner of the Broken's mouth curled into a smile. "Unless you are here to dine with her."

"Just ate." His hand went lower, closer to his weapons.

"Fed huh? Then you will be a tasty taste for Mother. We won't have to give up one of our own again for protection."

As the Broken tightened his fist around the wrench, his eyes sized him up and occasionally darted to what lie behind him. He shifted his weight and began to raise the arm wielding the wrench.

In one swift movement the sawed-off was out of its holster, and the ringing boom echoed through the halls. The attacker was flung backward, a hole ripped open in his chest. Blood and chunks of flesh spun off until they collided with the wall and floor.

The roar of the gun still echoed off the walls when the attackers from behind slammed into him. One leapt onto his back and tore at his face, while another sunk a knife into his wounded leg. Something also struck him in the side, next to his right kidney.

Dropping the sawed-off, he reached up with both hands and grabbed the attacker on his back, flipping him over his head and slamming him into the floor with a crunching sound.

Another blow struck his side, this time a bit higher, where his right arm connected to his body. He pivoted on his unwounded leg and saw two more of the sub-humans, one male and one female.

Both were unkempt and unwashed. The male had a section of metal pipe, long enough it had to be wielded with both hands. The female had the knife, which she raised to her lips. Despite looking to be about eighteen under all that grime, she had no teeth as she snaked her tongue out to lick his blood from the weapon.

As the man moved in to attack again, the Covered Man raised his pistol. It kicked in his hand, another boom echoing off the walls of the abandoned school. The projectile tore through the man's heart, his blood spattering the female next to him as he tumbled to the floor. She shrieked with anger, the remains of her companion covering the side of her face.

As she lunged forward with the blade, the Covered Man grabbed her extended arm with his free hand and applied pressure till he felt both of the bones in her forearm snap.

She dropped the knife to the floor and went mad with pain. She slammed her head into the wall twice, staggered in a circle and then ran off down the diagonal hallway. A slight rumble shook the floor.

The Covered Man stood for a moment. He took the clip out of the pistol, saw only two bullets left, shook his head, replaced the clip, and then placed the pistol in his leg holster.

Limping over to the wall, to apply pressure to the wound in his leg. The suit had already closed over it, yet he could still feel his life pouring from it. He wished he know why his invulnerability had been slipping away. With a simple thought the suit receded, revealing the stab wound.

No time to worry about that now, he thought to himself as he removed a needle, thread and a roll of bandages from his belt and started sewing his wound closed.

The Broken he slammed into the floor earlier yelled, "You! You! You will end up a treat for Mother! Hear me! Hahahah!" He tried to reach toward the Covered Man's leg, but it appeared his back had been broken when he connected with the floor.

The Covered Man finished stitching up his leg and wrapped a clean bandage around it as his suit again healed itself. He then strode over to pick up the sawed-off, dug out a new shell from his belt, loaded it and placed it back in its place on his belt. Only six shells remaining, along with a single makeshift explosive device Rays gave him. His puns were awful, yet one could not deny his tinkering ability.

"Hey!"

The Covered Man peered in the direction of the shout. The degenerate with the broken back squirmed and wriggled on the ground, trying to reach out and grab him but his damaged body would not respond.

"You have no chance! Mother will get you! Stronger now than when she first came here. Digging tunnels in your brain and burrowing deep into your inner most thoughts and memories! Then in Her wickedness, she will use those very memories against you!"

The Covered Man limped to the Broken, making sure not to put too much weight on his wounded leg. When the prone figure tried to claw at him, he swatted the other limb away with his fist. Shifting weight to his good leg, the Covered Man placed his wounded leg on the Broken's chest and leaned on it. The bestial man went crazy, screaming in pain as he felt the air being pushed from his chest.

"Looking for a type of engine, err, machine. Maybe yay big," he said as he held his hands about two to three feet apart. "Might be two of them, might be more." He leaned a bit forward again. "Intact BeforeTime technology."

"She will peel your mind back like peeling the paint chips from a decayed wall! Hear me!?"

"Can hear you all the way to the Shallow Sea. Where to find them? Leave you alone. Promise."

"Downstairs! Downstairs. A room filled with ancient mysteries. Things of another age. You will never get them, though. She guards that room. A lure for filth like you. I will laugh when she devours you. As you slip down into the abyss of—"

The Covered Man stomped on his face, cracking the Broken like a rotted pumpkin. After he scraped his boot on the tattered shirt of the dead man, he walked down the hall toward the hole in the floor.

"Downstairs, huh? Thanks."

Making his way to the section of collapsed floor, the light from outside found it more and more difficult to illuminate the gloomy interior. The Covered Man reached up and touched the edge of his goggles. The vision flicked, and the world switched to a luminous green taint. With the dark interior now lit up, it allowed the Covered Man to see into the shadowy corners. The indicator in the lower corner of the goggles flashed ninety-seven percent.

"Hmm." Once again, he had to give credit to Rays tinkering ability. Constructing a charging battery from what he scrounged up was impressive, given the limits of scrap that could be scrounged.

He leaned on the wall as he placed his weight on his good leg to squat down and sit on the lip of the pit. Looking down, he saw the half-collapsed hallway below. Directly underneath was the corpse of a woman.

Only bits of flesh remained attached to her body. A few strands of her light brown hair clung to her scalp. Black, thick-rimmed glasses lay nearby. The tatters of her remaining clothes showed some sort of grayish business attire. Her left arm and anything below her mid-thigh were also missing.

As the Covered Man climbed down the piles of collapsed rubble, he could see the tatters of clothes had something odd about them. When he reached the floor, he crouched next to the body. Her clothes were slightly burned, as if by a powerful acid. Continuing to inspect the body, her bones were marred by tooth marks. Some rat sized. Some human sized and some were unidentifiable.

He stood and rechecked his weapons. Still only six shells and two bullets. Replacing the pistol, he kept the sawed-off in hand. Glancing down both ends of the hallway with the goggles, he saw that the hallway to the left had collapsed, but the hallway to the right was clear.

Heading down this corridor, he soon came to slight turn to the left and a T intersection. A nearby metal door had a thick blood smear across it, appearing as if someone had run a blood-soaked hand across it.

With his free hand, the Covered Man shoved it open. He rapidly pointed the sawed-off around the room and glanced up at the ceiling. Once he was sure the coast was clear, he crept into the room as quietly as he could with his wounded leg. The room looked to be some kind of maintenance area. Racks for tools and benches lined the walls but the room had been picked bare.

Another metal door lay on the opposite wall. A few objects were piled in front of it, along with two heavy boards nailed into the concrete walls to keep it shut.

He put his ear to the door thinking he would hear more of the Broken shuffling about inside. Instead, only the oppressive silence touched his ear. He removed the debris from in front of the door as quietly as he could. Making sure to keep an ear alert for any kind of noise.

Not hearing anything out of the ordinary, he proceeded to dig the tip of a bar under the edge of the boards across the door. Rot had started to set in the wood so it peeled away easily.

Pulling open the door, the first thing the Covered Man noticed was another hole in the floor. This was not like the collapsed floor. This hole was almost a perfect circle. A few boilers lined the wall to the left. Straight ahead was yet another door, this one smaller.

The Covered Man skirted the hole and gazed down into it. The sides were smooth, with an almost machine-like quality to them. The top edge had crumbled away a bit. It gave the impression that the hole had begun to collapse, and then the hole had been 're-bored' again and again as the years passed by.

Reaching the door, he tried the handle. It wouldn't budge. It was slightly bent inward, as if something heavy had pushed on it. Numerous scuff marks could be seen along the edge where the door met the frame, showing many visitors had tried to pry this portal open since the BeforeTimes.

The Covered Man inspected the lock. Placing the sawed-off in its holster, he grasped the handle again and with a twist of his wrist, he snapped it off. Using his finger, he poked part of the lock mechanism into the interior of the room.

A familiar voice came from behind him. "Murderer."

He turned and saw The Ant Queen standing a few feet away. She looked like she did when they were part of the same team in the BeforeTimes.

"Hurt, you fuck. You destroy everything you touch."

The Covered Man turned back to the door and kept wriggling his finger inside of it to get the last remains of the lock out of it. He felt a slap on the side of his head. This time he spun fully around.

"You muscle bound fool! Why didn't you keep your nose out of other people's business?"

"Yinny's business?"

"Not her! You know what I mean! What you did! You should be dead after the crimes you committed!"

"Crimes to who? You? What things became?"

"You are the worst of us! The worst of humanity!"

"You care? Your daughter buried you under a hill. Along with yourself."

The Ant Queen screamed and raised her hand to strike him, this time she faded away into nothing as her hand was about to connect. The Covered Man stood there for a second, unsure if he just saw what he saw. Only a ringing in his ear where he had been struck gave him reason to doubt.

Another moment went by and when Anne did not reappear, he went back to the door, this time pulling the broken door open. The interior was some kind of storage closet. The shelves were lined with tools from a different age. At the back wall, his goal: two intact generators, both almost in perfect condition.

A rotted corpse lay in the center of the floor, about the same age as the one he found under the collapsed section of hallway.

This body was almost fully intact. Worms and maggots had finished off the flesh, but her skeleton revealed this was a young girl. He guessed in her late teens. The top of her head was missing, and in her hand she still clutched the pistol that he assumed she used to kill herself.

As he reached down to pick up the gun, he saw the extra underdeveloped skeleton in her abdomen. Trying to pop open the clip, the rusty weapon resisted. He kept looking down at the dead girl.

Why would a girl in her teens, and a young mother at that, kill herself? He guessed this happened during the actual Collapse. Many people took this way out rather than face what the world had become. He didn't blame them. Was the apparition of Anne somehow connected to this? Or did whatever make the apparition come later? Did this girl have a connection to the apparition, to the entity the Broken above spoke about?

This was not the time to ponder such things. He tossed the pistol aside; it was useless and the ammo useless from age. His priority was the two generators. The living had precedence over the dead these days. But he looked down at her one last time and swore if he could, he would retrieve her corpse and give her a proper burial in Blac Arth.

Lifting one of the generators to his chest, he carefully stepped over the girl's remains and left the storage area.

"Now you are sentimental?" Standing ahead was Judge Centurial.

"You want to bury a poor girl," the Judge stretched his arm around the room, "yet what happened to that girl, all of this. This was because of you."

"Hardly. Blaming someone lying in the sun for getting a tan is foolish."

"You know that is a lie."

"Know you are 'Mother' or whatever the Broken spoke of. Sees into people's minds. Pulled Anna and the Judge from my thoughts." He began walking forward, walking through the apparition with his precious prize. "You Devour. Do horrible stuff. Blah blah blah."

He walked into the next room when he heard the voice from the past say, "Damn you!" He heard the familiar blast of the weapon the Judge used to use, and felt a sharp pain in his back, hurtling him and his valuable cargo to the floor.

He flipped onto his back as quick as he could, sawed-off in hand. But no one was there.

Weapon arm extended, he sat for a moment. Nothing else moved. He used the generator to push himself to his feet. The pain his leg caused him was worse than ever. It was ignored. He had to get the generators to Blac Arth. If the fledgling town was to make it another year, they needed the additional power.

Being careful of his bad leg, he lifted the generator again. Glancing about the area to make sure no one else was there, he made haste to the hole in the floor by the front doors, all the while, looking around making sure no new specters from his past made an appearance.

With a single grunt, he lifted the generator through the opening and onto the floor above. Hauling himself up afterwards.

Stepping around the Broken who had greeted him, he stopped to turn off his googles so he wouldn't be blinded in the noon-day sun.

'Ninety-two percent left." He grunted in a statement of satisfaction.

He crossed the ancient parking lot and quickly stored the first generator safely in the black car.

One more and he could leave this place behind.

As he slammed the car door to head back into the building, the ground shook once again, a bit more violently this time. Once the ground stopped shaking, the Covered Man limped as fast as he could to get back inside to grab the last generator.

Adjusting his goggles once again to light the dim interior, he stepped over the two bodies of the Broken in the entrance. Two? Somehow that didn't seem right. Was there supposed to be three? Yet there were only two bodies there. Maybe he had been mistaken.

Jumping down again into the collapsed section of hallway, a large smear of some clear-ish gel coated the floor ahead of him. Something else was here since the last time he came through. But how could it be? He saw the clear slime right there. Maybe it had been there earlier. Was the pain from his leg causing him to neglect his surroundings?

His wounded leg must be worse than he initially thought, not to mention the headache he had for days now. Was it days? He seemed to remember it being a while, yet a small voice in the back of his mind poked at him. Something was amiss. Trusting that voice, he scanned the area for anything out of the ordinary.

The blocked hallway, the collapsed floor, everything seemed to be as the last time he passed through. Even the rotted body of the woman with the missing limbs was still there. He paused. He could have sworn something else was there a moment ago. What was it? He could not recall.

This bewilderment made the Covered Man's skin crawl. He needed to hurry and grab the last generator and get out of here.

Trekking down the corridor, he again reached the T intersection. He recalled there was a door here, yet he saw nothing.

Looking down the corridor to the right, he saw another collapse, but there was a door on the left side of the wall. Opening the door, he saw a small room. Sections of the wall and floor had collapsed and a few tables and chairs were tipped over and scattered about the room. A few chess pieces and boards were also strewn about.

What did he come in here for? The Covered Man glanced again about the room. He knew he was looking for something, but could not remember what. Knowing he was not looking for chess pieces, he turned around to leave.

The corridor was not empty this time. A humanoid figure was there with glowing yellow eyes. It appeared like a heat shimmer above blacktop on a hot summer day. The figure floated a few inches above the ground.

The figure spoke. "Feeling lost?"

"Professor Gravity? How…?"

"Fool. I am the force of gravity itself. You cannot stop me that easily."

"Snapped your neck. Stopped you…dead."

"Murderer! You are the one who should be stopped. You destroyed civilization as we know it!"

"Who cracked North America? Killing millions?"

"Those vile uneducated degenerates? Society is better off without them!"

The Covered Man walked forward. "Better off without sociopaths like you." He passed through the image as he said it.

Looking over his shoulder, the image had vanished. Turning his head forward again, he saw a metal door in the hallway he just came from. Why he didn't see that earlier he wasn't sure. Limping to the door and entering the maintenance room again, the Covered Man felt a moment of relief; he remembered the area correctly and no ghosts from his past floated around.

Crossing the room, he entered the boiler room. This area looked the same as well. Boiler. Big hole in the floor. Storage room entrance on the far wall. Making his way across the room, to the storage space, he saw the dead young mother, the rusted pistol and all the tools hanging on the walls, everything but the second generator.

Shaking his head, he wondered if he had even seen the second generator. Stepping forward, he waved his hand around where he thought he saw the other generator, but his hand connected with just air.

Another voice spoke from across the room.

"When you have eliminated the impossible, whatever remains, however improbable, must be the truth."

The Covered Man stood up straight, "No Face?"

Turning around, he saw his old ally. He was dressed in his typical dark brown fedora and trench coat, but without the jet black suit, the same type of body suit the Covered Man now wore. The bare ebony skin of his face smiled at him.

"Good to see you, son."

"Thomas. You don't have…"

"The second skin? I gave it to you, remember? So you could do… what you needed to do."

"What was it that I needed to do?"

The Covered Man looked down at his hands. He no longer wore the black body suit. As he looked back to No Face, he now wore it.

They stood on a rooftop in the city. The smell of pollution, sweat and dirt touched his nose.

"What? What are we doing here?"

The building shook under his feet. He extended his arms out to balance himself, certain that such a tremor would send the building collapsing to the ground. When it didn't, he lowered his arms a little but not all the way, still wary.

No Face did not seem fazed by the quake and started walking around the rooftop, motioning the Covered Man to follow. "Don't you remember? The League of Madness is attempting something that will shake the world to its core."

He tried to keep up with his old friend, but for some reason his leg twitched with pain. He couldn't recall how he injured himself. "Do we know what they are attempting? Seems I should know, but I cannot remember."

The pair of them came to the edge of a small platform above them. No Face jumped up to catch the ledge and pulled himself up. No Face crouched down by the ledge to indicate the Covered Man needed to jump up as well. "You do know. It's what provokes you to do what you did."

The No Longer Covered Man attempted to jump to the ledge but again, pain shot through his leg. He stumbled, but No Face grabbed his hand and pulled him upwards.

Getting to his feet, he seemed confused. "What I did? I don't understand. How can the League do something that causes me to do something I haven't done yet?"

No Face walked forward. On the platform there was an upraised part with a door in the side. He headed straight toward it. It must be the doorway to the building's stairwell. But why would No Face use the stairwell? His old friend usually used a grappling hook and rope to get around to avoid running into civilians inside buildings.

"It is amazing that fate has delivered you here to me. Once we are done, endless knowledge of The Was will be opened. Maybe the secret of my own origin will be known."

No Face reached the door and opened it. Standing aside, he beckoned him to enter.

"Your origin? We always knew your origin. You were fed up with how things were. It was mine that we only had theories about."

"Yes, you are right, of course. But all will be revealed once you enter."

He took a step forward.

A boy and girl stood in the doorway, holding hands. The boy was thin and nerdish looking, the girl had blonde hair and also had the same geekish look to her.

The boy said, "Are you ready for immortality?"

The girl beckoned to him, "Immortality. We are together forever here."

"When you join us," the boy added, "we can look into you and you into us, all of us striving for the same goals. Can't you see the wisdom?"

The girl said, "All of us. Together. Can't you see the wisdom?"

His mind burned like it was on fire. The pain made him feel like the front of his brain was going to burst out of his skull.

"Ah! Thomas! Run!"

As he looked at his friend, the world changed, like someone threw a light switch. One moment he was on a rooftop standing next to his friend about to enter a doorway to a stairwell. The next he was in a ruined school. No Face was nowhere to be seen; he again wore the black second skin. The doorway remained but instead of a stairwell on the other side, there was a large chamber, like a gymnasium or an auditorium.

In the center of that open space, was a worm, maybe twelve feet in diameter. It had human-esque lips. Its maw was open, showing numerous human teeth, each about the size of his head, lining the interior of its mouth, like a lamprey.

In an instant the worm lunged forward to devour him, smashing down the doorway and collapsing the section of wall around it. The disfigured lips wrapped themselves around the Covered Man, trapping its next meal inside of it. The Maw Worm smiled with its victory. Ready for all the knowledge this newest feast would give it.

It swallowed.

Confused, it swallowed again.

It reeled back, tearing out a large chunk of the concrete wall in pain.

The human-like mouth opened wide in an inhuman scream. Never in its many years of existence had it felt such pain.

The Covered Man landed on the floor. Patches of the second skin had burned away from the acidic spittle, revealing pale skin that had not seen the light of day for years. His suit was trying to repair itself from the acidic saliva. In his hand he held a molar the size of a human head, the roots still dripping blood. Two more of the uprooted teeth clacked across the hard floor.

"Legged vermin! You are not fit to accost me! You are only fit to embrace eternity!"

It opened its wide mouth again, this time the mouth lined with its own blood. The Covered Man dropped the tooth and let loose with his sawed off shot directly into the soft skin of the inside of its mouth.

The volume of the shotgun blast was rivaled by the bellows of the Maw Worm's shriek of pain. It reeled upward in pain, its head smashing into the ceiling, knocking large chunks away. Some of them pierced the Maw Worm's flesh.

A few chunks crashed down on the Covered Man. He managed to dodge the first but with his wounded leg, he couldn't twist fast enough to miss the second. It clipped him in the shoulder, hard enough to dislodge the sawed-off from his grip, sending it clattering across the floor.

"You are the destroyer, all right, human. But I am the devourer!" It again opened its mouth to suck the Covered Man into its gullet. Using his good leg, he pushed himself backwards, out of the way of the worm but away from the sawed-off as well.

He drew his pistol and fired both rounds into the side of it. No effect. The hide was too thick. The only way to injure it was a shotgun blast to the inside of its mouth, and his shotgun lay about twenty feet away. He glanced at the dropped weapon and calculated how fast he could reload it.

"What's the matter, my brother of the BeforeTimes?" The Maw Worm drew back, snake like, and smiled an inhuman smile. Blood dribbled from its lower lip. "Seems you are out of pellets for that weapon. You have ammo for the other, yet it lies out of reach. Too bad."

Its smile grew wider, this time showing its human-like teeth, along with the gap. "Why don't I give you a sporting chance? Your leg is wounded is it not? Go ahead. Get your gun. Once you do, only then I will attack."

The voice of No Face echoed in his mind, "When you have eliminated the impossible, whatever remains, however improbable, must be the truth."

The Maw Worm said, "That is fair. Yes?"

"Eliminated the impossible, whatever remains, however improbable."

"Yes?"

"Improbable."

The Covered Man leapt toward the fallen weapon, clumsily stumbling with his wounded leg. The Maw Worm snapped downward, anticipating where the Covered Man would be mid-leap to finally devour its prey.

Instead, as the inhuman mouth descended down upon him, the Covered Man did the unexpected and reached up to grab where the worm's upper and lower jaw met. Using his good leg, he kicked the Maw Worm as hard as he could in the lower lip, using the momentum to propel himself onto the thing's back.

The Maw Worm probed his thoughts, and discovered what its planned meal was attempting to do and screamed, "No!"

From the thing's back, he withdrew the cobbled together explosive that Rays gave him and climbed through the rupture in the ceiling, throwing the grenade into the space between the roof of the building and ceiling of the gymnasium.

The explosion rocked the building, sending parts of the structure earthward.

When the dust settled, the Covered Man found himself laying on a pile of what was left of the roof of the building, now resting on the gymnasium floor. He listened to the hollowness of his breath, gazing up through the hole he created at the broken waxing gibbous moon.

The pile lurched and heaved, as the Maw Worm began to struggle. Twisting and heaving to try and free itself from under the tomb of metal and concrete, "No. No! How can this be?"

Grasping onto a metal beam, the Covered Man pulled himself to a standing position. Then staggered over to the shifting pile, and removed a large slab of debris, revealing the remains of the Maw Worm.

Greasy blood and ichor coated everything. Part of its head had been torn away, where the ceiling struck it. Revealing some grayish bundle that pulsed and writhed almost as much as the rest of it.

It faced the human that now stood over it, its bulk shivering as it read the others thoughts.

"No! Stay away from me! I am immortal! I am eternal!" It pressed its lips against the floor to attempt to burrow away, but its head snapped back in pain. "Aah!" Its cried, "My missing teeth!"

It attempted to shrink back underneath the collapsed ceiling as if could somehow hide its massive bulk, "Stay away from me!"

Ripping one of the thinner metal beams from a nearby pile, he stood over the creature for a moment; then drove the end of the beam into the exposed brain of the Maw Worm, like a macabre St. George.

A wave of mental force struck the Covered Man so hard he had to hold onto the beam so he did not get pushed away.

"You! You are the monster! Unlocking your mind I know exactly who you are! What you did!"

Raising the fragment of metal above his head again, he stabbed the entire length of it into the worm until only the few inches of it that he grasped remained visible.

Then retracting the metal object, he drove it back into the creature again and again. The Maw Worm tried to twist and buck to knock its attacker away, but with a large section of it still pinned underneath the heavy sections of the ceiling, all it could do is yell in terror until it stopped moving.

"Yeah. But you're dead."

With one last jab, he once again buried the fragment of metal so far into the thing's brain, only an inch of it remained visible.

The Covered Man stretched out his hand to steady himself for a moment, and then began to pick his way across the uneven sections of floor.

He didn't even attempt to look for the sawed-ff. He could dig for ages and never find it. The only thing that mattered was finishing his promise and get back to Blac Arth.

Enough of the torn-open doorway was left to allow him room to squeeze through, making sure he kept his most recent wound from scraping against the dirt. Hobbling to the hole in the corridor, he gingerly held his side as he made his way back to the bottom floor and then to the maintenance storage room. He staggered a bit, from the loss of blood, and his injured leg would need to be re-set most likely.

Just as he suspected. The second generator was where he had left it. The mental powers of the worm had only made him think it had disappeared.

As he prepared to hoist his treasure and carry it back to the black car, he saw the remains of the young mother and child. The Covered Man stared at them a few moments, hands still firmly grasped around the generator.

He was in no shape to make two trips and he knew it. Didn't he promise he would bring back both generators? He set the generator back down and placed rags and junk he found around the room on top of it. Grabbing an old blanket from a storage shelf, he carefully placed the remains on the blanket and gently wrapped it up in a bundle. Holding it in a protective way to his chest, he made his way back to the black car.

STORY FIVE

Cold days of Blac Arth

The fallen leaves of autumn danced around the barrier walls of Blac Arth. The occupants expanded the fortification of ruined vehicles in the prior months, to extend three blocks east and ten blocks south.

They had guards posted at even intervals along the walls while other settlers gathered whatever leaves they could to mix into the dirt of the fledgling garden. If everything worked out, Blac Arth would soon be on its way to self-sufficiency.

The two generators from the school hummed behind the metal barrier in The Shop. Mattresses and old cloth lined the surrounding walls to buffer the noise.

An assembly was being held in the garage of the old firehouse across Canal Street from The Box, and southeast from The Shop. Once the old fire engines were moved out and became part of the western wall, the firehouse became the new headquarters of the town. Its solid brick foundation made it even more formidable a structure than The Shop. It was perfect for storage of food and scarce materials, and for town meetings.

Joshua stood on two tables pushed together. Most of the other settlers crowded around him as he was discussed the pros and cons of stringing permanent lights around the settlement. It would help them see danger further away, but would attract more raiders and mutants.

A lone, brutish man leaned against one wall like a statue, his goggles taking everything in. Only an occasional turn of his head showed he remained amongst the living. While listening to Joshua's speech, his mind drifted to the past.

It had been three months since he returned with the generator and the remains of the nameless mother he found at the old school. She was the first person they buried in the new graveyard across the highway. Upon returning to the settlement, he collapsed and remained bedridden for almost a full week and a half.

Sike and Javier took the truck and, using the Covered Man's directions, located the other generator and brought it back. Despite his warning, they snuck into the old gymnasium to see the remains of the Maw Worm. Its massive bulk was rapidly decaying, and they could see very little of the carcass under the blanket of flies covering it.

With both generators retrieved, Blac Arth had lighting in The Shop and refrigeration in The Box. The refuge had grown into a home.

The Covered Man snapped out of his thoughts. He explored much of the area in the past months, including opening trade with the settlement of Sawksity to the north. Despite endless skirmishes, Fappa Jack and his gang remained a problem.

'The 14' had to be patrolled constantly, especially to the northwest, the direction most travelers came from. There were enough people and makeshift vehicles to make this happen. When the Covered Man found the multiple abandoned fields of corn to the northeast, Rays built them an ethanol tank. They had to be cautious with its use, but they now had limited fuel as well.

The meeting continued. Marta, one of the newcomers, replaced Joshua on the table. She was talking about how they needed more power for day-to-day things. As the residents discussed things they need for this or that, the Covered Man felt his mind drift. The wind rushed through his hair as he leapt over skyscrapers. His skin repelled everything from bullets to lasers to deadly radiation.

Then the screams began. Screams of anger. Screams of pain. Screams of terror. Screams begging him for life.

The echo of the screams in his mind snapped him out of his thoughts. Seeing no one noticed he dozed off, he detached himself from the wall and made for the hallway leading outside.

Once again, he wondered if he should just load up his car and go wherever the road led him. Being part of such a large community still made him uneasy. He knew if he left, Fappa Jack, the mutants, and who knows what else would tear this place apart.

Why did he care? Searching his thoughts, he could find no answer. For one who had answers for most things, that was disturbing.

As he pushed open the door into the crisp, early autumn air, he felt the hands of his past push him to leave this settlement and relegate the doomed residents into memory.

"I knew you wouldn't sit still that long." Kristine sat on his car, smiling. "Where you off to today?"

"South. Jack's been quiet lately."

"Are you going to let me come with you?"

Kristine anticipated his answer, and at the same time, they both said, "No."

Kristine added, "Come on! Manny has been teaching me to shoot. He says I have a natural talent for the rifle."

"Then stay here. They need a sharpshooter on the barrier."

She folded her arms. "Humph. I am not moving. You need to take me with or–"

With one arm, he hoisted from the car and placed her to the ground. "Or I can leave without you."

She put her hands on her hips as he got into the car. "You're an asshole."

They spoke in unison again. "Yeah."

The Covered Man revved the black car to life and headed toward the gate. Monnic, a boy of eighteen who just came to the settlement a week prior, stood atop the gate with Dor. When the Covered Man honked, Dor waved at him and pulled a lever. Gears engaged, and the gate opened with the sound of metal grinding on metal.

With the gate open far enough, the black car sped through it and into the southern ruins of Blac Arth. Dor and Monnic watched the vehicle speed off.

The newcomer turned to Dor, keeping his eyes on the vehicle receding into the distance. "Guy's really a super?"

Dor nodded, "Sure as I am standing here."

"Thought they were all dead."

"Same. But you missed a helluva fight between that guy and Fappa Jack's best. Cracked his skull like an egg."

Before they could continue their conversation, another engine roared to life behind them, deep inside the settlement. As they turned to the sound, one of the recently repaired dune buggies zipped around a corner and headed toward them. Kristine was behind the wheel; a rifle on the seat next to her.

Dor smiled down at her. "Your dad know you're stealing one of his buggies?"

"Not stealing. He said I could take it to go hunting."

Dor smiled and shook his head. "Hunting what? Alone?"

Monnic said, "Want me to go with you?"

Kristine set her jaw firmly. "No. I can do it myself. Open the gate."

Dor already had the lever in hand. "Don't wander far by yourself. And don't go after *him*."

"After who?" She asked, then put on protective goggles to keep the wind from her eyes. When the gate hit its zenith, she revved up the engine and drove through.

"You're just going to let her go through?" Monnic asked.

Dor nodded. "She's got a good head on her shoulders. Not to mention she is one of the most stubborn human beings I ever met."

Monnic just stared.

Dor mulled for a moment as he watched her speed into the ruins south of the settlement. "Go run and tell Rays. We can send an extra patrol after her just in case."

As the youth sped off, Dor felt his pocket to make sure it was filled with ammunition.

The wind whipped Kristine's long black hair around her face as she watched the road ahead for any sign of the black car.

I will show him how valuable I can be. He will see how much he needs me in his life. She swerved around debris on the side of the road. The past few months were a constant struggle with Fappa Jack over the stretch of highways around Blac Arth.

A shred of doubt crept down the back of her neck. She recalled when the stranger came to Blac Arth. He became a rock they all clung to; a living artifact from the days humans ruled the earth.

The fear that he could leave at any time and things would go back to the way things were always lingered in the back of her mind. Starving. Cold. Scared. Things were safer with him there. And he needed them. Her. Something obviously troubled him, and she could fix him.

She had watched him closely the last few months as he lived among them. He rarely talked to anyone, interacting only when something needed to be done. He gazed off into space, and then snapped back to reality, haunted by some demons only he knew. She needed to save him, to make sure their guardian angel always stayed with them. With her.

Kristine raced on for at least thirty minutes with no sign of the stranger. Deeply in her thoughts as she sped down the highway, she didn't see the ambush that awaited her.

With a roar of an engine, a car covered in rusty armor plates pulled out from a side road with two other vehicles behind it. The plated car smashed into the dune buggy, flipping it over and over like a tumbleweed. After rolling down a small embankment, the buggy came to a final resting place upside down on the edge of a small creek.

Kristine lay dazed on the ceiling of the vehicle for a moment. Her head throbbed as she tried to regain her bearings. The sound of cars stopping and idling nearby was replaced by a crescendo of howling raiders as they ran down the embankment.

"Get away!" Kristine cried as the raiders shrieked with perverse glee and stormed the side of the overturned car.

A raider with blue hair reached the driver's side. He grabbed her leg and pulled on it. Wagging his tongue, he giggled, "Ooh, a fresh one!"

Another, wearing a football helmet, gazed at her and licked his lips. "Nice and juicy! Cannot wait to sample her."

Another raider reached the side of blue hair, his face painted with red stripes and piercings covering his nose. He shouted, "Hey! Hey, Megmas. It's her. The delicious flower Jack wanted to pluck."

A low, garbled voice called from up the embankment, "Is she alone?"

Red Stripe looked inside the vehicle. "Yeah, she's alone."

Megmas laughed. "Rays let her wander? No, more likely she snuck off. If we return her to Jack, he'll let us snatch our goodies. Drag her out of there. And don't worry about being gentle, just make sure she's breathing when you're done."

Kristine's heart was already racing, but it threatened to burst after hearing that. At least seven raiders were gathered around the car, all pulling at her. She lost her left boot and her pants started to tear. She scrambled for anything she could get a hold of.

She managed to grab a metal bar of the buggy's frame. She kicked wildly, feeling her feet connect with flesh but not stopping to check with the results. She spasmed and contorted; anything to keep her attackers away. As her fingers began to slip from the buggy's frame, she flailed with her free hand for anything to anchor herself. Her hand grabbed something cold and metal, but not sturdy enough to hold her weight.

The Rifle!

She grabbed it and twisted, pointing the barrel blindly toward her feet, and braced the stock against her armpit. As she pulled the trigger, she pulled her feet back and much as her attackers would permit.

The bullet tore through the face of the blue-haired man, right below his eye. Pieces of skin, blood, and the cloudy contents of the eyeball spattered across the face of the raider next to him. Both shrieked, and one fell to the ground dead. All the raiders let go and retreated from the buggy.

Megmas' shouted, "Hey! Hey, flower. Don't be like that."

Katrine screamed back, "Stay away from me! Leave me alone!"

"Deary Dearest. You can't fight this. We have you. You cannot look every direction at once. What will you do for food? Sleep? Fleshy leakage?"

Kristine looked from the driver's to the passenger's side, trying to keep the rifle at the ready. One raider peeked around the corner of the passenger's side, near her head. She fired the rifle. The bullet tore through space and ricocheted off the vehicle's frame. Despite missing her attacker, they did not reappear.

Megmas mocked her. "Tsk. Tsk. A rifle only holds so many shots. Another thing not on your side, my glistening raindrop."

"The Stranger in the black car is right behind me. He will be here soon, and he will kill all of you!"

"This is why you will be better off with us. You won't be able to spit all those lies from your pretty little mouth. It will be busy elsewhere." A wave of giggles and chuckles rolled through the raiders. "The black car went southward a few minutes before you. Were you chasing him, my fairest bird? Maybe to give yourself to him? Neither of you will snatch what you were hoping in your net today. You will end up in our harem, and the Owl won't find Jack. The boss should be descending on your precious Blac Arth as we speak to burn it to the ground. Your father's head is probably already on a spike!"

"What? No!"

An arm clothed in denim and rags crept in from the driver's side. A hand covered in a rawhide glove struck out and grabbed her ankle. She turned and fired, but the arm had already withdrawn. More laughter rolled through the air.

Kristine sucked in quick, short breaths as she tried to look in every direction at once. The denim-wrapped arm appeared again to grab her foot. She fired, and the bullet went straight through the jacket sleeve. The force of the bullet knocked the glove from the arm, revealing the trembling tip of a tree branch.

She realized the deception too late.

Rough hands grabbed her and pulled her from the vehicle. In her panic, she tried to wheel the rifle around as fast as she could, but it struck the frame of the buggy. As raiders swarmed over her, one of them grabbed the barrel, tearing her last hope away from her.

"No! Please!" she cried in vain.

The raiders tore at her clothing. Her belt and other boot were forcibly stripped from her. Multiple hands roamed over her body, exploring her every curve. Tears welled up as they tore off more of her clothing.

A raider sauntered around the side of the overturned vehicle. Ebony skin covered his muscular form. A full clown mask with no pigment left on it covered his head. He wore leather pants with boots that came up to his knees. A slightly curved sword hung from his belt. Kristine assumed this must be Megmas.

He stood over her, undoing his belt buckle. "Jack'll only get mad if you're violated in certain ways. There are other ways to—"

The roar of a shotgun filled Kristine's ears. Everyone stopped to turn in the noise's direction. A raider slumped against a tree, his face a shredded pulp. He glanced about with his remaining eye and tried to open what was left of his jaw to scream in pain.

Above him, replacing a shell in a sawed-off shotgun, stood the Covered Man.

The raider holding Kristine's leg let go and raced toward the figure in black, drawing a knife. He received a fist between his eyes for his effort, hurtling him to the ground.

Hands released Kristine as they went to their weapons. She crawled away, trailing torn bits and pieces of her clothes behind her.

Megmas growled, "You! How did you—"

The Covered Man raised the sawed-off and pointed it at Megmas. "Car's leaking oil. Followed the trail."

Megmas grabbed a raider in a football helmet and pushed him at the Covered Man. The raider flailed his arms wildly, trying to grab hold of anything to stop his fall. With the roar of the sawed-off, the chest of the scrabbling raider exploded. Chunks of flesh, lung, and entrails spattered those who stood near him an instant before his shredded intestines poured out onto the grass.

The remaining five raiders drew weapons and opened fire at the Covered Man. He ducked behind a nearby oak tree as pellets of metal sent bark exploding where they struck. The Covered Man reloaded the sawed-off again. When finished, he withdrew the knife from his belt.

Megmas buckled his pants while shouting over the gunfire, "Hey! Owl! You shouldn't have interrupted us! Now you will die, and Jack will still get his prize!"

Kristine gasped and tried to get to her feet while grasping the remains of her clothes close to her. Before she could stand, Megmas pounced on her like a wolf spider catching its prey. Grasping her wrist, he dragged her toward the vehicles.

"Help me! Help me!" Kristine cried.

The Covered Man tried to peek around the side of the tree, only to have another onslaught of ammunition rip into the side of it. Two raiders broke off to flank either side of the tree with pistols held out in front of them, like a priest would hold out a cross to exorcise a demon.

This demon heard the screams of Kristine recede as she was dragged away. He realized he would have to do something drastic. If Megmas got away, he would have to make it all the way back to his car. Who knew what could happen to Kristine in that time.

He stepped out from behind the tree, flinging his knife into one of the raiders. It split his nose in two and buried itself up to the hilt in his face. A bullet caught the Covered Man in the side. He felt it pass through the meat of his shoulder and agony lit up his mind.

Whirling around with the sawed-off, again his old friend kicked, roared, and spat its cargo of metallic shot into the raider coming around the other side of the tree. The sheer momentum from the blast sent the attacker careening to the ground, his weapon hand torn to pulp.

Bullets flew by the Covered Man, one getting dangerously close to his head. He threw the sawed-off like a knife at Red Stripe, one of the three raiders that remained. Startled and thinking it was another knife, he dodged into a female raider's line of sight, who lifted her weapon just in time to avoid shooting him.

Legs that once could jump a half of a mile with ease launched the Covered Man at the one raider still pointing a weapon at him. He held his hand out in front of him, ready to stop the bullet so it wouldn't hit anything vital.

Instead, the raider turned to run. The Covered Man used the momentum to slam his fist into the back of the man's head, shoving him into the overturned dune buggy. With a clang of skull on metal, the man fell to the ground, unmoving.

The other two regained their composure and bore down on him again The Covered Man launched himself in a new direction, putting the remaining man between the female raider and himself.

As the female raider moved to the side to get a better shot, the Covered Man's boot connected with Red Stripe's groin. The force of the blow carried through the flesh as the air filled with a crackling of bone within.

As the man wavered, the Covered Man pushed him into the female raider, sending them both to the ground. She pulled the trigger as she fell, but it went wide.

The Covered Man leaped into the air and came down on her skull with a sickening crunch.

He did not pause to survey the carnage, check his wound, or even retrieve his knife or gun. He raced after Megmas and Kristine. He caught up with them just as Megmas finished tying his belt around

Kristine's wrists and threw her in the passenger side of one of the raider's cars.

"Stop!"

Megmas turned. "I figured with all the shootin', you were tearing through those grubs."

"Not done yet."

Megmas backed away from the vehicle, ready to gamble for his life. With curved blade in hand, he said, "Oh really? As we speak, Fappa is burning your precious settlement to the ground."

"Lies." The Covered Man stepped forward, raising his hands, ready to crush the life out of Megmas.

"Am I? Why do you think we were watching the road? Better hurry or your new home will be ashes." Megmas smirked and spun around to run.

The Covered Man knew if Megmas was telling the truth, he would not have time to retrieve his car. He reached the passenger seat and freed Kristine from the leather strap.

She gazed up at him, his goggles reflecting her shame back at her, deepening the wound of her recent assault. He stepped away from the passenger seat and motioned to her, "Drive."

"What? No. I can't."

He moved to the back of the car. "If Jack is attacking, all will die. Drive." He found a handful of metal spears and a hockey stick with a saw blade attached to it. He gathered them up.

Fear gripped Kristine tight. Tears trickled down her face. She could barely stand upright. Her father, Linda, Joshua who took them in. All of it might be lost, swept away as if by a giant hand scattering dust. She hated this world. How unfair it was.

The Covered Man stood by the car. "Hurry. Every moment could be folks' last."

Like a zombie, she shuffled over to the driver's seat. The Covered Man climbed in as the vehicle roared to life.

"Blac Arth will be ash if you don't hurry."

Kristine snapped, "Stop! Just stop! I was assaulted!"

The Covered Man grabbed her by her shoulders and put his face so close to hers that she could see the details of her eyes reflected in the goggles he wore. "Drive!"

Kristine pushed her foot to the floor, and the tires kicked up a cloud of dust and pebbles as the car sped off.

"Why are you so mean?" Kristine wiped the sweat from her brow. "You lived with us for months, and yet you never talk to us or interact with anyone."

The Covered Man's silence gave her courage to prod more.

"If you didn't like us, you would have left us by now."

The figure in black just sat there, staring forward. If his hand didn't shift to hold onto the spears as she hit a curve in the road, he might have been a statue.

Kristine shouted over the thunder of the engine.

"Talk to me!"

The Covered Man kept his goggles focused on the road ahead of them.

"Blac Arth's in danger."

"You're always are rushing off somewhere! My dad idolizes you! He constantly says your coming to our settlement was like some kind of divine saint arriving or something. But you do not even talk to him. Not even a 'Hello' or 'How's your day?'"

After a few moments, the Covered Man spoke in a voice that left her colder and feeling more alone then when she was hiding in her crashed vehicle and Megmas and his thugs planned unspeakable things for her, "Drive. Or you'll drive back alone."

"But…"

The Covered Man began to open the door, even as the buggy sped along.

"Okay! Okay."

He swung his foot back inside and closed the door, readjusting the spears against the car door.

Roaring back to life, Kristine put the car in motion again. Almost a full minute went by before the one of them said something, "No Face," the Covered Man said. He no longer stared at the road, but at the dashboard. Focusing on a point far beyond it, in the knotted cobwebs of his mind. His grip on the weapon and the spears eased up as well.

"Huh?"

"No Face. When I started out, taught me… lots. Police procedure. Detective skills. Like a father."

Kristine shifted her gaze from the road and the figure sitting next to her. "What happened to him?"

He once again snapped to attention and focus on the road.

"What happened?"

"Almost to Blac Arth. Jack and his raiders lying in wait. If there."

Kristine sped forward. The burned out skeletons of homes dotted the right side of the road. She only knew them as relics, things from another age. The stranger held the secret to what happened the world. Right now, her mind focused on trying to get the stranger to Blac Arth to save it.

When ruins appeared on the left side of the road, two motorcycles, each with a single rider, and a car loaded with at least six raiders came from a side street - the rear guard to a raiding party.

The Covered Man edged his bulky frame out of the passenger side window, sitting on the door. He withdrew a metal spear, ready to strike.

The first motorcycle pulled alongside them, trying to match their speed, the second motorcycle a half a bike-length behind it.

"Hang on!" Kristine shouted. She jerked the wheel to the right, but the first cyclist dodged the sideswipe. The cycle behind them did not anticipate the maneuver.

Trying to avoid being struck by the buggy, the cyclist swerved and drove into the loose gravel on the side of the road. The motorcycle veered back onto the road, close enough for the Covered Man to slam his fist into the man's jaw, forcing him into the ditch. The bike struck the uneven ground and flipped over, sending the rider flying off to collide with a burned out oak tree.

The car laden down with raiders nudged the car Kristine drove, trying to cause her to spin off the road. She tightened her grip to keep the car steady, watching for another opening to strike.

The three vehicles passed a sign reading 'F KP' that marked a road that intersected 'the 78'. There, two more cars laid waiting.

One of them tried to pull into front of Kristine, but she jerked the wheel to the left and smashed into it with such force that fragments of broken glass and metal scattered across the road and the raider's car spun off onto the side of the road. The collision slowed her vehicle and tore off some of the armor on the front of the car, exposing its innards.

Seeing an opportunity, the cyclist veered to the other side of the car. Raising a hand crossbow, he prepared to fire it into the exposed engine.

The Covered Man launched a metal spear through the air, piercing the cyclist's body. He coughed blood once, and skidded off the road.

Not only ruined houses on either side of the road flew by them now, but the remains of old businesses as well, hinting they were approaching their settlement.

Withdrawing the second spear, he raised it, preparing to launch it at the driver of the vehicle filled with raiders. Fear appeared on their faces as they braced themselves for the incoming projectile.

A loud crack rang out over the roar of the engines and a sniper's bullet grazed the Covered Man's shoulder, causing him to drop the spear.

The raiders let out a yell of victory and pounded on the roof and the side of the car while hollering; preparing themselves to board the car Kristine drove.

The Covered Man looked down at his shoulder. It wasn't bad. It barely pierced the skin, but it still drew blood.

In the distance, he saw the building that he cleared of babblers a few months ago. From the left side of a cross street, a large red truck came straight for them. Fappa Jack stood in the back, aiming a mounted bolt thrower at them.

Kristine swerved to the right. The car with filled with raiders had to slam on its brakes to avoid colliding with the red truck.

The car with just a driver tried to brake as well. The momentum carried it into the back of the other car, forcibly dislodging one of the raiders. The raider bounced off the hood of the car and into the street directly in front of the red truck and disappeared underneath its tires.

The side street was narrower, and the pavement in such a bad state of repair, Kristine could not help but slow down as the car got jostled this way and that from the bumpy surface.

Kristine had to slow down even further since they reached a T intersection. Directly ahead lay a large one-story building that appeared to be made of concrete.

The Covered Man scrambled from the window onto the roof. Steel twisted on steel as the red truck slammed into the back of the car Kristine drove, sending it up over the curb, slamming into the concrete structure.

The Covered Man jabbed the spear into the hood of the truck and held on as it swerved to the left. Roaring toward the settlement of Blac Arth, its makeshift wall now visible in the distance.

Fappa Jack fired a volley of arrows from the device mounted on the back of the truck. The Covered Man flattened himself onto the hood, allowing the deadly missiles to pass overhead.

Militia on the wall opened up with pipe rifles, forcing the truck to take another immediate left onto another road, running parallel to the barrier.

Using the spear stuck in the truck's hood, the Covered Man pulled himself up to swing the hockey stick with all his might, connecting with the windshield. A cobweb of cracks spread out across the glass, but the stick snapped in half.

Thrusting the remains of it through the windshield like a jousting knight of old, he shattered the glass and pierced the driver through the chest, pinning him to his seat.

The driver slumped over, his blood coating the dashboard. The wheel jerked to the side with no one controlling it, flipping the vehicle onto its side. Metal ground on pavement as the truck slid across the broken road into the intersection in front of the gates of Black Arth. The Covered Man rolled across the ground before coming to a stop.

As the last car approached, his head spun while he tried to get his bearings.

The red truck lay on its side nearby. Fappa Jack lay next to it with blood trickling down his face, but still gripped the bolt throwing device He simply said, "Die.", then fired.

Only two of the arrows connected. One into the Covered Man's left shoulder, the other just below his right collarbone. The world flashed white with pain and he collapsed back to the broken street.

As he lay there, Fappa Jack struggled to free himself from the wreckage. The last car pulled up and numerous raiders spilled out and surrounded the Covered Man as he strained to breathe.

Jack screamed, "Beat him! Beat him until his brains spill out onto the road. Then we will hang his corpse here so Joshua and his lot can look at it every day until they join him!"

The Covered Man felt a boot connect with his ribs, and a section of metal pipe strike his leg.

Then a shot echoed through the air, and a raider, minus their head, collapsed onto the road in front of him.

The roar of two vehicles approached from behind him, the direction of the settlement. The attackers he could see backed away.

As the vehicles sputtered and stopped, Joshua said, "Jack. We gotta stop meeting like this."

"Yeah. This time your avenger is down. Dying in the street like a dog!"

The reply came from Manny. "Come on, Jack. Look at you. Down to one vehicle. Five followers. Face it, you're beat. Just move on."

Jack just stared, his hands balled into fists, ready to combat all of them hand to hand.

"Why do you care about this guy? Who is he?"

Rays shouted back, "He is one of us. He might be an anti-social jerk, but he's *our* anti-social jerk."

Manny struck a blow that rippled through all of them. "He is one of us more than you ever were. Not using fear and numbers for control. He taught us to stand on our feet, that we are not you."

Jack just stared, his hands unclenching.

"I protected you for ages."

"Kept us dependent on you for ages."

Jack slouched in defeat. He made a motion with his hand, and the surviving raiders clamored back aboard their remaining car. "You know what's coming, right? The Beast will tear you apart. Will tear *him* apart."

"We haven't seen or heard from the Beast for ages."

"Because I protected you!"

A long silence washed over those who faced each other in that intersection. Finally, Jack shook his head and walked to the passenger side of the vehicle. Half-climbing into the window, he said, "I will laugh at your corpses after the Madtowners tear this place out from under you," then disappeared inside the last car. Starting the engine, the last car turned around and sped southward.

They watched the car drive off.

Joshua said, "Get him on the truck."

The Covered Man felt multiple hands force him to a sitting position and Javier threw an arm over his shoulders. Rays did the same, as they gently hoisted him to his feet.

As he looked around, he saw all the original Blac Arthers there. Joshua, Rays, Dor, Sike, Linda, Javier, David, and Manny. Joshua still watched in the direction Jack drove off, but repeated, "Okay. Get him to the truck. We need to get him back to his cot."

As they got him onto the truck, Linda leaned over him. "Stranger. Where's Kristine? Dor told me that she followed you."

"Drove me back. Collided into building. East side."

Linda gasped, "We need to go get her." The Covered Man struggled to sit up.

Rays smirked, "Not you today, trash bag. You, my friend, are going home."

As he lay there looking up at the sky, he heard Joshua say, "Linda, you and Rays take Sike, Manny, and Javier with you to go find her. David, Dor, and I will take the stranger back."

Joshua said a few more things… but the Covered Man did not hear them. Rays' words echoed in his mind. He thought back to the BeforeTimes, to one called No Face, probably the best friend he ever had.

STORY SIX

Dreams Ended

The stench of burning human flesh permeated the air as flames from the dumpster leaped into the sky. A lone patrolman stood nearby, pounding a metal stake into the ground.

Similar stakes were evenly spaced in a circle around the burning dumpster. As the patrolman finished his work, he hit a button on top of the stake and a digital barrier floated in the air between them with red letters that read 'Police Barrier. Do not cross.'

Satisfied with his work, he took a step back to admire it, but bumped into something. Spinning around, he went for his pistol, but a strong hand grabbed his wrist. He found himself staring into a lithe man just short of six feet. The figure was dressed in a charcoal black trench coat with gloves, boots, and a fedora of the same color. No skin was visible on the figure. A material that was darker than the surrounding night cloaked the figure under the coat.

"Ramos". The figure in the trench coat said in an electronically modified voice.

Patrolman Ramos jumped in surprise. The black figure let go of his wrist. "Shit. No Face. Why you gotta sneak up on a fellow in the middle of the night?"

"It is 3:30. Hardly the middle of the night." He looked at the dumpster, still burning wildly. "What have we got?"

"A body. Set on fire. Enver ran off to find a fire extinguisher."

"Don't have one in the cruiser?"

"You know about the budget cuts?"

No Face nodded, "How's Enver's wife?"

"Due any day now. Checked her in the hospital yesterday morning."

"And you?"

"I am happy for them, but anyone who would want to raise a kid in this day and age is doopy."

A few people showed, curious about what was happening, but not getting too close because of the smell.

No Face said, "Keep them back. I want to investigate around the dumpster."

"No problem."

As No Face walked toward the dumpster, he added, "Have you or Enver gotten close to the dumpster?"

"You kidding? Some of us do not have a filtered suit like you do. That reek is horrible."

No Face walked closer to the burning dumpster as it spat ash and smoke into the early morning sky. No Face was not interested in the smoke. He kept his gaze on the ground, scanning around the metal container.

He saw what he hoped to find. A few footprints around the dumpster. Crouching, he took a vial from his belt and squirted it into the footprint. It became a thick foam and then solidified, giving him an impression of the footprint in seconds.

Hmm. Size twelve; some kind of work boot.

As he picked up the impression, he studied it further. The grooves along the bottom were hardly worn at all. Strange.

The familiar voice of Enver echoed from the walls, "Hey, No Face! Glad you're here. But you better be quick. City decs will be here any minute to investigate everything. I know you hate how they muss up a crime scene."

No Face stood. Enver kept a sleeve over his nose as he exchanged the shoe print for the fire extinguisher.

"How's the wife?"

"Good. She went to the hospital yesterday. Little Enver will be born any day now." His eyes watered as he moved back from the smoke.

With the grace of a swan and the precision of a tiger, No Face swung his leg over the edge of the dumpster. The intense heat did not faze him through the body suit—his own invention. But he had to work quickly to make sure his boots or coat did not catch on fire.

A thick sheet of foam burst from the extinguisher. The flames retreated, knowing their time had come. Smoke poured from the burning debris, but No Face could make out the remains of a human body, twisted in pain. It appeared whoever it was had been set on fire while they were alive and conscious, or they awoke while burning to death.

Tossing the extinguisher to the ground, he crouched next to the body. A few sparks flew up from where he set his feet on the burning garbage below him, desperate to cling to life a few moments longer, to no avail.

147

The condition of the body was poor. Almost all discernible features were burned away. The time the body was burning, plus to have it so thoroughly burned, some kind of accelerant had to have been used. Someone did not want this person identified.

Kneeling down, he placed a gloved hand on the corpse's head. Despite most of the ear being burned away, there were still a few metal piercings there. Bits of skull were exposed, charred black from the flame. He inspected this, then the jaw line. The rounded forehead and jaw identified the person as female.

No Face then used his thumb to pry open the mouth as wide as it could go. Flecks of burned skin crumbled away like one of the first snow flurries of winter. The third molar had grown in, but not all the way, identifying this person around the age of twenty-one or twenty-two.

Removing his hand from her mouth, he noticed an odd hole in her lower lip. Still mostly intact, he could tell there must have been some kind of piercing there as well, now removed. Where is it now? If it came loose, the lip must have been torn or burned enough to allow the jewelry to fall away. Yet, with the lip intact, the piercing should have still been there. Curious.

With a gloved hand, he pulled back her lower lip. The flesh was badly burned, but he found what he was looking for: a tear in the flesh. Someone had removed the piercing that was there by force.

Whoever killed her knew her. It was unlikely she was killed for the piercing. But the fact the murderer removed it, and not the earrings, showed that it had some kind of sentimental value.
Turning her head again, he checked behind the remains of the right ear to find her jack. A cybernetic implant the wired used to plug in data. Usually, a musical playlist.

But her jack was empty.

No way the data stick could have fallen out. One has to press and hold it in order for it to pop out. She was burned alive just for her music? He had seen stranger cases for certain, but No Face guessed there was much more to this.

Removing a small cylinder from his belt, he pushed it against the burned flesh from her arm. A small, steel bear-trap-like mouth emerged and took a bite out of the victim's flesh. A small screen on the side of the device flashed, "DNA scanner activated," along with a percentile number showing how far along it was in analyzing.

Around the thirty percent mark, the words flashed, "Unable to comply. DNA scrambled."

A DNA scrambler? Only the rich and powerful could afford such things. Why would the rich and powerful be in one of the worst slums of the city? How did they not get noticed? Even at three o'clock in the morning?

No Face spoke to the body, "Someone did not want you identified, that is certain, Jane Doe. But why?"

The cylinder finished its calculation and flashed the following, "DNA Test: Failure. Blood Type: A Negative. Substances found. Blood Alcohol level: .22. Legally intoxicated. Other chemicals found are as follows: Ko, Sixty-one percent. Most likely victim overdosed. Minimal Traces of accelerant. Most likely absorbed through the skin. Minimal traces of the substance: ICE, most likely absorbed through the skin."

He looked at the readout for a moment. Why would someone use both Alcohol and Ko? Ko was short for Knock Out. A depressant that has a similar effect as alcohol. So why take both?

I.C.E., Ixamethosone Chemdesivir Epitos, is a highly addictive drug, but why does she have it just on her hands and not in her system?

Digging into his belt again, No Face pulled out a small black box with several ports extending from it and a thin screen. He spun it in his hand to locate the port he wanted. He plugged it into the port behind the dead female's ear. After a second or two, the screen flashed, "Zhaji Component. Type: Dataport. Model Number: EL-07910330."

He stood, replacing his devices. Double checking to see if he had everything, No Face hoisted himself out of the dumpster. A group of almost twenty bystanders were now there. They all appeared as shabby and as rundown as the rest of the area.

Ramos and Enver kept the gathering crowd away from the crime scene. No Face walked up to them and took the shoe print back from Enver, tucking it in his coat.

Another car pulled up: the city decs. Most of them were puppets of the Ad-Hocracy. He felt lucky he got here when he did, otherwise the scene would have been compromised and the case unsolvable. He recognized the man and the woman in matching suits as they got out of the car, Ratto and Memm.

Both were overweight from sitting at their computers and not doing the legwork needed for good detective work. The fact they were there alone rose suspicion.

Enver asked hurriedly, before the decs were in earshot, "Who were they? Any ID?"

"Female. Early twenties. No trauma. Enough alcohol and Ko in her that either could have killed her. If there was an ID, it was destroyed in the fire. She was soaked in accelerant."

"Both Liq and Ko? Must have been a hell of a party."

"I suspect she was drugged so whomever did this had time to search her and then set this up."

"Set this up?"

"Are there other dumpsters around here? It's the middle of the quad. Someone drug the dumpster here to send a message to the residents, it would seem."

"Got an idea about the perp?"

By then, the two Decs were standing next to them. Ratto rubbed the stubble on his chin. "Go back down your hole, you costumed rat."

Memm popped some pills into her mouth. "What have you found? This is our district, No Face. These officers called it in to our station. If you contaminated the crime scene, you'll wish it was you in that dumpster."

"Your minds are not nearly as large as your stomach, and one of those is a lot emptier than the other."

"Why, you…" Ratto said. A flap opened on his wrist, ejecting a small laser into his hand. Memm raised a hand, her fingertips crackling with electricity—each a miniature taser.

Anticipating this reaction from the decs, No Face held a small disk in between his thumb and forefinger. Flinging it like a frisbee, it struck the wrist that Ratto held the laser in.

In an instant, the night lit up with a blue-white crackle that struck both of the decs. Ratto's mechanical eye cracked and his cybernetic muscles locked up, sending him to the ground. Each of Memm's fingertips flared for an instant, then burned out. Her enhanced, computerized brain also fried as a bit of smoke curled from her ear and she also collapsed on the ground.

151

Ramos took off his hat and ran his hand through his black hair. "You *do* know that EMP pulsers are illegal?"

No Face tipped his hat as he began to leave.

"Hey! You can't just leave. You need to tell us what you found." "Once those two get their implants repaired, they will be on you both with an endless stream of questions. I will contact you as soon as I have something."

Enver smirked, "You sure live dangerously."

Tipping his hat again, No Face added, "You will understand why once your kid hits the terrible twos."

The two plain-clothes detectives turned their attention back to their duties.

As he walked to his car, No Face thought about his next move. The first thing he had to do was find out who the victim was. With no ID, the best bet would be to trace the number of the data jack in the remains of her head. If he recalled, a Zhaji Outlet Store was only a few blocks away.

⭷⭣⭤

The store was about as run down as the rest of the area. Most of the sign on the front of the brick structure was faded, and numerous pieces of paper remained stuck to the building. Flyers for missing girls, pets, or where to buy drugs hung there. Some half remained from people trying to tear them down.

Most were just covered up with newer flyers, the original victims forgotten about.

The door to the place had bars over it. That would be no problem. The trick would be if he could crack the digital lock before

152

the alarm system discovered him. An EMP disk would also work here, but he would have to use one so powerful, it might fry the electronic devices inside, destroying the reason he was there.

As Ramos said earlier, EMP devices were highly illegal. When over half the city's population was wired with anything from silicon muscles for enhanced strength and reflexes to digital minds that allowed them to think hundreds of times faster, a simple device that made those advantages into disadvantages was not popular with those in charge.

If you do not have any superpowers, trying to win a fight or catch one was difficult, if not next to impossible. The EMP rendered them helpless.

The wired didn't realize when they became 'enhanced,' they crippled themselves forever. But most of the wired were not the smartest people, either.

The outlet's interior looked little better on the inside. He pulled a pair of goggles from his coat and lifted them to his eyes. They stuck to the material of his suit. Reaching up and clicking a button on their side, the night vision came on and he could see as clear as on a summer's day.

He looked up and saw the cameras, but ignored them. The suit he wore came with camera scramblers, making him appear as just some static on screen.

The floor was heavily stained. The ceramic tile was cracked and broken in many places. Many of the devices on the shelves were in poor condition, even if technically they were brand new. The boxes had crushed corners, some had water damage, and others were as faded as the sign out front.

Along the back of the outlet lie the object of his search. A computer terminal on an old counter. Striding over to it, he pulled another cube from his belt, this one labeled "LightningBolt" Plugging it in, he booted up the computer.

Text flashed on screen: "Welcome to DMALeech. The most frequently used passwords on this device are: MastaMo454, Teepz9$, HotAzz@$$." He pulled the device from the machine and rebooted it. Trying the MastaMo454 password worked.

A screen appeared with the Zhaji logo on it. Beneath it, a drop-down box said, "What Can I help you with?" He clicked it and selected "Part numbers". The new screen asked, "What is the part number you would like to search for?" After typing in EL-07910330, the screen switched.

The new screen had a picture of an attractive young woman in her early twenties. She had long blonde hair done in side-swept style. She had the same number of piercings in her ears as the body he saw earlier. The image had a golden heart piercing in her lower lip, right where the hole had been. Dressed stylish, but trashy.

The text on the side of the screen read: Jenna Alhubru, ID: Zo-Zo. Address: 716 Fifth Street. Apt. 19-99.

716 Fifth Street? That was the same complex where the body was found. Was she taken from her apartment, or killed on her way home?

No Face searched through the computer more. If Jenna had come into the shop, there should be video of her. Everyone was documented everywhere those days.

Discovering the video of her transaction, he brought it up. She entered the shop with a smile on her face. No Face wondered if she knew whoever was working here that day, since her mannerisms suggested familiarity. Once she made it halfway across the room, the video abruptly ended.

Curious, He thought to himself.

He fast forwarded the file to the end, but the entire transaction was static. He surmised that someone had erased it. But who? With a few more clicks on the keyboard, he brought up the employee manifest. Eleven people worked there. Twelve if you count the owner. Quite a few for such a rundown shop. Hard to believe they made enough money in this part of town to have so many employees.

He brought up another video from a similar time that day. It was also erased. Strange. One final thing to check, he tried to bring up a schedule for who worked what hours, but could not find one.

It seemed people worked whenever they wanted at Zhaji Components.

Pulling the box from the port, he popped in a storage device. He dragged the video of Jenna to his storage drive, as well as a copy of the business transaction. If someone from this shop was involved in Jenna's murder, it would help to have proof she was here before someone could delete it. He took the storage drive from the computer and shut it down.

One last thing to check, the video of the installation area, where people get their implants implanted. Strangely enough, there was no video footage of the implantation area. Usually, this area was where they have the most cameras to make sure no one sued for liability if the implant went wrong or the techs botched things.

In the installation area, No Face found a number of shoes and boots there, all pulled apart like dissected frogs. Both Male and female models.

He pulled a chip detector from his belt and waved it around the room. Any electronic device with microchips in them—anything from computers, to tools, to cameras—would set it off. It made a warbling noise similar to sonar.

As he pointed it toward the electronic devices used to do the implants, is emitted a higher pitched tone. As he pointed it away from them, the tone softened.

The pass around the room took about ten minutes. He carefully inspected every device the detector found. No cameras. This meant that illegal chip implants were being done here. He made a mental note to return here once Jenna's murderer was found.

No Face wandered back to the street, making sure to lock the door behind him. He thought about Jenna's data jack. He had suspicions, but no proof.

He only made it five steps from the building when the familiar visage of Axiom drones approached in their familiar triangular formation.

"By the license of Axiom, prepare to be scanned."

The lead drone detached itself from the group and hovered a foot from No Face. A flickering blue light started at the top of his fedora and finished at the end of his trench coat.

"Subject: Thomas Farewell. Code Name: No Face. Height: 175cm. Weight: 88kg. HQR Code scanned. Authorized."

"Pleasure to see you Axiom." He lied, "What could I help you with at this hour?"

"Please inform what you were doing in facility Block 37, Building Y59, Licensed to Zhaji Components?"

No Face had to be careful about lying to the computer that controlled most of the planet. Everyone knew someone that lied to the Axiom AI. None of the stories had a happy ending.

"Investigating a call at 716 Fifth Street. The inquiry brought me here."

"This case was assigned to officers Joens Ratto and Miriem Memm. They already closed the case as a random homicide. Relay to us what have you discovered."

No Face rubbed his thumb and forefinger together. What he said next might get him erased. If Ratto and Memm reported his use of EMP charges, he might be erased faster than that.

"The victim's name was Jenna Alhubru. She lived in the same apartment complex where the body was found." Taking a deep breath, he added, "I agree she was just a victim of a random robbery. Nothing of value was found on her."

Seconds ticked by. He could feel the Axiom AI checking his heartbeat, analyzing his voice for any anomalies that showed his deception. He hoped that the black suit he created would continue to mask this.

"Next course of action?"

"Investigate the victim's apartment. To discover and notify any next of kin." It wasn't a lie, but it was not the full honesty either.

"Negative. Officers Ratto and Memm have already contacted the next of kin. By the order of Axiom. This case is closed."

The leftmost Axidrone hovered closer to him and a presented a data port to him, "A datacube has been detected on your person. Please upload its contents."

No Face knew if he plugged in the cube, the Axiom AI would know everything he found inside the store. He also knew if he didn't he would be killed on the spot.

He plugged in the cube and after ten seconds, the Axidrones popped it back out.

"Please retrieve your cube. Contents erased for your protection."

No Face replaced his now blank storage device into his pocket.

"File your report as soon as possible. Have a good evening Subject: No Face."

No Face watched them fly off. *How much did Axiom AI know? It was almost as if the drones were waiting for him. Did Ratto and Memm mention his EMP usage?*

Climbing into his car, the next stop would be back to the complex where Jenna's body was. No Face suspected Ratto and Memm would be gone. They didn't care about the murder of some low-life. Needing repairs would take precedence over solving a case. Only crime that got them in good with the Ad-Hocs were worth their time. With the loss of everything on that cube, it was the only lead he had left.

By the time he pulled up to the quad, the burning dumpster had been extinguished, as well as the interest of the two decs. As suspected, their car was gone. In their place was an ambulance. Two EMTs spoke to Enver and Ramos. One or two bystanders remained, but everyone else had wandered off.

No Face got out of the car and approached. They all turned to look at him. The two officers were indifferent, they knew each other well. But those from the ambulance looked at him with disdain.

One of the EMTs asked, "A supe? What is he doing here?"

Enver said, "Hey, No Face. You uncover anything?"

"Yeah. Victim's name is Jenna Alhubru. Twenty-one years of age. Lived in the far side of this complex."

Enver replied, "I know her. A doll. She's been busted a few times for love brokerin' without a license. No drug use, yet."

Ramos said, "Yeah? If she was burned here, maybe a message? Gang hit?"

No Face rubbed his chin, thinking about this new information, "Maybe Jenna knew something she wasn't supposed to know? Or maybe she got too greedy."

The two EMT's folded their arms, unhappy a super was at the crime scene. If they reported his being there to the Axiom AI, he would have real problems.

He turned from them, head tilted downward, deep in thought about the ramifications of what he just discovered. While facing away from them, he still tipped his hat. "Thank you for your assistance. Best wishes again to you and your wife, Enver," and began to walk away.

One of the EMTs behind him said, "I cannot believe you let a super interfere."

Ramos replied, "No Face isn't like the others. He must have been a lawjock once. He does a lot to help the community."

No Face blotted the rest of the conversation from his mind as he strode across the quad toward Jenna's apartment. What was Jenna doing at the Zhaji Outlet? Did she know about the lack of camera installation? Was that why she was there? What did a simple Love Broker need there? What was the relation of the golden heart piercing?

Striding between two buildings, He looked for any marker on the buildings to orientate himself. Determining that the building on the right was where he wanted to go, he slipped in a side door. He paced himself as he climbed to the nineteenth floor. Upon reaching it, he took a brief rest before cracking the door and peering through it. Once he determined the hallway empty, he strode as smooth as a lover's whisper to the door with a 'ninety nine' above it.

It was locked. He leaned toward the face recognition reader, and once it scanned the suit, the door clicked open.

The place was in disarray. Someone was there already, searching for something. He pulled the chip finder from his belt and scanned the room, although he was sure any phones, computers, or other electronic devices were long gone.

Someone had torn apart the main room even worse than the entry hallway. The couch was flipped over and cushions torn apart. Everything seemed rummaged through. In the bedroom, condoms laid open and used on the floor. Upon inspection, the semen was dried. Most likely from a visiting love seeker, not from the recent intruders. The bed was also torn apart, the mattress searched. Various sexual paraphernalia lie strewn about the floor as well. One nightstand was completely smashed, and nearby laid a nu-lamp, also broken. Shards of it littered the floor.

As he passed back through the main room to the kitchen, he spotted a picture on the floor. The plastiglass was broken. It was a picture of Jenna with an arm around a man. He appeared to be half Asian. The man was familiar looking. No Face could have sworn that he was a spitting image of a man who worked at the Zhaji outlet earlier that evening. Curious. He carefully worked around the fractured plastiglass and removed the photo. Flipping it over, he found a message scrawled on the back in poor handwriting. "Love ya! —Masta Mo."

He thought for a moment. There was a Masta Mo on the employment roster of the outlet store, along with an address. It seems that would be his next stop. He folded up the photo and pocketed it.

Continuing his trek to the kitchen, the chip finder buzzed ever so slightly, then stopped. The tone didn't even change pitch. It happened so quick, No Face wasn't even sure he heard it. Leaving nothing to chance, he swept it back over the position it had been in just moments before. It took a bit of finesse, but there was something, however faint.

The most prominent object nearby was the hutch the visiscreen rested on. It was smashed like everything else, along with all its little nick-knacks. The chip finder buzzed louder as he passed over the broken objects. One of them was not what it appeared to be.

No Face zeroed in on a collection of fractured figurines lying about a small ceramic house with a shattered roof. It set the chip finder ablaze. Picking it up, he found a micro-camera inside a window, about as large as the head of a pin.

Not a strong device. Whoever was on the other end lived somewhere nearby.

He crushed the house in his hand and picked through the pieces for the camera. Pulling a thin wire from the chip reader, he plugged it into the micro-camera. The camera was transmitting to somewhere. With the chip reader attached, he should be able to follow the signal back to its source. He waved it in the air. It pointed upward.

Before No Face followed his electronic bloodhound, there was one last thing he had to check. Searching the kitchen and bathroom, he discovered paraphernalia for chem usage, as he suspected he would. On closer inspection, he identified bottles for Love Juice and a few syringes marked for Sharp, but nothing for Ko or ICE.

He closed the door behind him as he made his way back to the stairwell. He followed the signal up two more stories. The other end of the signal was in apartment 21-01.

Pulling another device from his pocket as wide as his hand and just as flat, he pointed it at the door, each residency on the planet was uploaded into a database. So certain people could keep track on where you were at any time. The reader read off: "Tene Fenway. ID: Skann. Address: 716 Fifth Street. Apt. 21-01. Currently under investigation for drug abuse and Love Brokering without a license. Currently lives alone."

He returned the device to the pocket he pulled it from and knocked on the door.

A woman in her mid-thirties opened it. It looked like she slept little. She did not seem to be surprised to see him, and fear had drawn heavy lines across her face.
"What do you want?" She barked.

"What happened in Jenna's apartment?" No Face asked.
"Who? I don't know what you are talking about?"

He leaned in. "What did you see? Her place was torn apart." He held up the micro-camera. "And I found this camera in her apartment. A camera that led me directly here. Jenna was murdered recently in the quad, a stone's throw away from here. A camera leading directly here doesn't look good. It is a level one crime for a non-corporate to spy on others. Unless…"

Tears poured down the woman's face as soon as he mentioned 'corporate'. She rubbed her eyes, smearing bits of her cheap mascara and leaving serpentine trails across her cheeks. "You found out! I didn't mean to see what I did. I just was keeping an eye on Zo-Zo. She was my friend, really. I was worried about her."

"What did you see?" No Face asked again.

After a moment of sniffling and dabbing her eyes with the sleeve of her shirt, she regained her composure. "I… I don't know who they were. But they came in… maybe between three and three-thirty. At first, I thought they were love seekers. You know, because Jenna is a…"

"I know what she was. Continue."

The women looked visibly shook as he referred to Jenna in the past tense. "They trashed the place. They looked like the Ad-Hocracy. Y'know, the Corps. What would they want with Jenna? If they killed her and find out I saw them, I'll be next. I'm next!" She broke down again.

No Face felt for the woman. Life as a love broker was a tough one. He knew from growing up on the streets. But he also knew that if Ad-Hocs were involved, this went deeper than he realized. Anyone caught even touching this spider web would surely be snapped up and eaten.

He pretended like he knew nothing about her, "Look, uh…"

She looked up and stared into the infinite black of his suit. "Skann."

"Look, Skann. I won't lie to you. If corporates are involved in this, we are both in terrible danger. But if I can discover who killed Jenna, maybe we can hide your trail so you will be safe." Of course, he was lying. If the Ad-Hocs got a whiff of anyone breaking their rules, their lives were over.

"I need a drink." She turned around and went deeper into her apartment, then set down a small bottle she was holding on a table in the hall. She flicked a few lights on as she went. She must have been sitting here in the dark, terrified for her life.

Picking up the bottle, No Face saw it was for ICE. She must have been coming down from a state of euphoria. Makes sense why she still opened the door. She must have been out of this world.

"How did you get a camera in Je—Zo-Zo's apartment?"

In the kitchen, Skann pulled a bottle of Gray World Vodka from a shelf and poured herself a glass. "We both work in the same field. She was stealing all my clients. I used to have love finders lined up down the hallway every night. Now, I get maybe one call a week." She gulped down the contents of the glass in one swift movement.

Alcohol *and* ICE.

"No one liked Zo-Zo. She was cocky and arrogant, like she knew something everybody else didn't." Skann set the glass back on the counter but brought the bottle with her as she walked out into the main area and flopped on the couch. "Seat?"

"No thanks."

"Suit yourself." She took a swig directly from the bottle. "I wanted to know her secret. How did she steal all my business? I know she's wired. Did she get implants everywhere? Was she part bot? Those lousy bots were stealing most of our business. But I figured I could find some incriminating evidence on her, turn her over to you people, and get my 'fans' back while she did time. Or maybe I could learn how she did it so I could try to get them back that way."

"How did you get the camera in her place? It doesn't sound like she would invite you in for tea."

After a heavy sigh and another long swig of liquid courage, she said, "Vaypa."

"Vaypa T?"

"You know him? I suppose you would."

"He has been busted many times for ICE possession, and dealing. You wouldn't know anything about that, would you?"

She looked away, staring down the long barrel of the bottle. "Vaypa would do anything for ICE. I got him ten jems of it, and he lent me his key to Zo-Zo's apartment for an hour."

"Why did Vaypa have a key to Jenna's place?"

Skann just shrugged, "Maybe she brokered for him? He is the Love Biz for lots of other dolls. Although, I saw Jenna running together with Vaypa and his unders. Not together together, the Love Broker way. Like she was his equal." She mumbled the next part under her breath, but the chems in her system allowed it to slip a little louder than planned, "Think she's better than me..."

Skann caught herself from speaking the rest of that thought, "I hid the camera in there and have been spying on her since." She looked up. "You aren't going to bust me, are you?"

"How long ago did you hide it?"

"About a week ago. Hey, I don't use the stuff. I just got it for Vaypa so I could hide the camera."

"Where is Vaypa these days? After his last arrest, he vapored."

"Aw, man. First the corps, now Vaypa! My life won't be worth an asshair on an alleyway rat."

"This might be the only way to save your life."

Skann peered into the rapidly emptying bottle. "18 Terrace Avenue, Street, fifteenth floor, only apartment on the floor." She tilted the bottle to her lips and drained the remaining contents with a few gulps. "Now, please leave me alone."

No Face reached into his pocket, retrieved the picture he took from Jenna's apartment, and handed it to Skann. "Do you know this man?"

She shook her head. "I've seen that picture in Jenna's apartment. But I've never seen him visit."

"Are you positive?"

"Yeah. I'm sure."

He folded the picture and put it back. "Do you have anywhere you can lie low for a while? I wouldn't stay here."

She stood and wavered, the alcohol seeming to take effect. "Yeah, with another doll, er, love broker, Swalla. Lives a few kilos from here."

No Face turned to leave. As he passed the table with the empty ICE bottle, he picked it up and placed it in his pocket. He retrieved a credit stick and placed it where the bottle used to be. "For the ride to get out of here. If I see you again, and you are still shooting ICE, you are going to be charged." He tipped the brim of his hat. "Thank you for the information, it was very helpful."

Walking back to the stairs, No Face pondered his two leads. The man from the picture, Masta Mo, was also on the Zhaji outlet roster. And Vaypa T. He had arrested Vaypa T before, so he decided to check his place first.

The wind whipped at No Face's trench coat as he climbed up the side of the apartment building. Gusts were determined to detach him from the surface and send him plummeting earthward. The fabric of the suit made sure nothing like his hat or things attached to his belt would be blown away.

Reaching the fifteenth floor, he perched on a window ledge. He had memorized the floor schematic he downloaded, and this was the guest bedroom for Vaypa's place.

From surveillance, he knew Vaypa had a few female guests this evening, but they would not be staying in the *guest* bedroom. Putting his back to the wind, he removed a small device and shook it. One end glowed white hot, and he placed that to the glass. He drew a circle wide enough to crawl through, and the glass melted away at the device's touch like melting ice.

Putting the small rod back on his belt, he stepped through the hole. The glass had already solidified, no longer hot. He stood for a moment, listening to make sure his entrance was not detected. The only noise was the whip of the wind outside. For all the residents knew, it could have just been a window left open. Satisfied he was unnoticed, he removed his goggles from under his coat and put them on, turning on the night vision. He double checked the digital map. The bedroom was the next door to the left.

He cracked the door open and could see a few of Vaypa T's gang in the main living area, playing Call of Duty Forty Five on their digital visiscreen. The area was well lit, and numerous guns lay within reach. *So much for taking them out quietly*, he thought to himself. This would make things a bit trickier.

A small voice in the back of his head screamed he should abort this mission. But he knew with the hole in the window, he would not get another shot at this. He would have to wait until Vaypa got caught again, and he did not have that kind of time to waste.

The area was cloaked in shadow, allowing him to creep out of the guest bedroom and next door to the master bedroom.

Locked, of course. An old-fashioned style lock. No electronics at all. Pulling a thin, flat piece of wire from his coat, he slipped it between the door and the frame. After a few prods to locate the spot on the mechanism he needed, a soft click emitted from the lock as it gave up the contents within.

He gazed over his shoulder as he returned the lockpick to his pocket. It seemed none of those in the other room heard him.

Slipping into the room, he saw an immense master bed, almost as wide as the room itself. Three figures were asleep on it. Vaypa T and two females, one on each side of him.

He removed a vial of foam glue and squirted it into the seam between the frame and the door. It wouldn't stop the gang members completely, but it should give him time to get answers.

He turned back and approached the bed. Clothing was scattered around the room. There were three sets of shoes there, with two female pairs, around sizes four and five. The male shoe was size eight.

The tread on the bottom differed completely from the prints outside the dumpster. The dirt on the bottom had already dried. It was unlikely that Vaypa wore any other shoes that evening since he most likely did not leave this room after he removed his footwear.

No Face crept to the left side of the bed to check the nightstand for weapons. Passing by the window, he placed a small explosive on it. He hoped he wouldn't have to use it, but this wasn't the most ideal situation. As he grasped the handle of a nightstand drawer, the nearest woman's eyes popped open.

"Wake up! Wake up!" She whipped the covers aside, and lying in between their naked forms were a few pistols and a needler. She grabbed one and pointed it at No Face. He slapped the gun away as she squeezed the trigger, and a bullet tore through the wall behind him...

He slammed his fist into her nose. Her head snapped back and she slumped onto the bed.

The other woman leaped from the bed and ran for the door, screaming for the rest of the gang to come help. When she reached the door and discovered it wouldn't open, she called for help and pounded on the door.

Vaypa grabbed the needler, "Face yo, Scag! Why yo here? I gunna—"

No Face jumped on the bed, kicked the needler from his hand, and kneeled over him. He grabbed Vaypa's hand so he could go for the other gun. Then he grasped the cybernetic implant around Vaypa's right eye and pulled on it. Vaypa screamed in pain.

"Ahh! You chuz! You fuckin' chuz! What you want? I done nothin' wrong!"

Using his thumb, No Face pried open Vaypa's eye. "Eyes are swollen and red. Your skin is oily. Looks like the symptoms of heavy ICE abuse."

The woman's pounding on the door was matched by angry shouting and pounding from the other side. Time was running out before the door gave way.

No Face grabbed Vaypa's ocular implant and twisted it again. "Jenna Alhubru. How do you know her?"

"Ahh! Stop, you ball-lickin' chuz! Don't know da betch!"

No Face pulled on the implant, nearly ripping it from the man's face. Vaypa screamed and clawed against his grip, kicking his legs wildly.

As No Face let up the tension, Vaypa caught his breath and spat out, "You sonofabetch! I'll fuckin' kill you."

Shaking his head in dismay, No Face pulled again, this time rising to his feet while holding onto the implant, pulling Vaypa off the bed.

Vaypa screamed again, and those on the other side of the door pounded more frantically as they attempted to break it open.

"Okay! Okay! Jenna's one'a my dolls! You wanna finance some clock with her? You could use da relax, chuz."

"Rumor has it, she has been buying ICE for you. Since its most likely not your birthday, why? And how is she getting that much ICE for you on a love broker's cash flow?"

"Maybe she just a hard workin', dedicated doll? Usin' her pie to get that American pie!" Vaypa laughed. No Face released the thug's hand and slammed his fist into Vaypa's face while pulling back on the implant.

"Jenna be protted by now! Not my fault she dead. The Ad-Hocs came by earlier tonight! Dumped a bundle so we stay on the lockdown. Said Jenna's marked for liftin'."

"Lifting? Did they say who she was stealing data from?"

"No input, chuz! Gave us cred to have a wild time. Who I to say no? Dey just barked, 'Stay on the lockdown.' Weren't no quizzin' from us. No way I pissin' off the Ad-Hocs. They not just kill you, but will wipe your digisistance. Like you ne'er were!"

No Face knew it was time for him to go. The door would only stand a few more moments, but there was something else he had to ask. He reached into his coat and withdrew the picture of Jenna and Masta Mo.

"You know this man?"

Before Vaypa could answer, there was a white hot blast from the door. The plasma flames melted half the woman who stood near it in an instant. Vaypa used the distraction to place his bare foot into No Face's chest and kick him off. As No Face tumbled off the bed to the floor, Vaypa grabbed the needler.

"Fire! A full stack goes to the brahbrah who kills that doopy chuz!"

No Face leaped to his feet, not even going for his pistols. He knew he was completely outgunned. He pulled a small sphere from his coat and tossed it at the door. He flinched as needles pierced his back and bullets tore through his right arm.

Charging at the window as fast as his legs could carry him, he hit the top button of his coat with his good arm, blowing the window apart a fraction of a second before he dove through it.

Vaypa yelled something at him, but the wind rushing by him in his plummet earthward drowned it out. He unhooked a small box from his belt, tapped a button, and braced himself.

A small grappling hook launched into the side of the building and held tight, a coil of cable spiraling after it. No Face gritted his teeth a second before the cable became taut.

He jerked like a marionette as gravity tore his arm from its socket. The cable swung him into the building around the third story, battering him against it.

He let go of the grappler and his dislocated arm flopped to his side as he held onto an outcropping with the other, causing jolts of pain from the bullet wound. The limb became unresponsive an instant later, sending him tumbling to the ground below and driving the needles deeper into his back.

Lying there on the ground, No Face gazed up at the morning sky. He knew the path this case was taking him on, and he could not do it alone. He propped himself up on his right arm despite the pain from the gunshot, since the other dangled uselessly at his side, and pushed himself to his feet. The tear is his suit revealed the wound in his ebony skin for a moment before the suit began to heal.

Staggering to his vehicle, his mind raced wondering who he could call for assistance with Ad-Hocs. They owned everything and everyone in it. Not just above the law, they *were* the law. As he got in his car, he realized there was only one person he could trust.

But that alone was a risk.

>米<

No Face slept most of the day on a shabby couch. The apartment he found himself in looked worse than Jenna's in some ways. Chinese food containers and empty beverage bottles lay strewn about. Some were stacked in patterns, apparently to see how high they could go before they toppled.

"Feeling alright, Thomas?"

No Face realized his mask was off, laying on a nearby end table. As he sat up, he also realized his arm had been popped back into place, an ice pack had tied over it.

"How long was I out, Hurt?"

"All day. Showed up here and flopped down like a gutted fish."

"You always were eloquent with words."

The brutish man shrugged and finished whatever he was doing in the kitchen. Cooking something with real meat, by the smell of it.

"Where did you get—"

"Beef? My secret. What about Maggie? I was gonna call her and let her know you're okay, but I forgot the number."

No Face did not want to talk about his problems. Maggie had taken herself and their son Jayce to live with her mother a week prior. She said it was because he was a super, but he suspected much more.

"It's okay. She knows I am on a case. She's used to me not coming home for days. You know that."

"Uh huh," Captain Hurt said as he entered the main room. He set a piping hot mug on the table next to No Face's mask and sat in the easy chair next to the couch. His frame was so big, it appeared like a man sitting in a chair built for a six-year-old.

"Drink."

No Face took the mug and sipped from the piping hot container. Genuine beef stew. It tasted amazing as the broth passed his lips.

"Where did you ever get beef?"

The other man just stared at him with a piercing gaze. "What case brought you to my doorstep in such wonderful condition?"

Setting the mug back on the table, No Face slowly reached into his coat pocket, wincing in pain as he did. He pulled out the photo of Jenna and Masta Mo and tossed it to Captain Hurt.

"She's cute."

"She's dead. At three thirty this morning, she was found burning in a dumpster. An accelerant was used to make sure it was a thorough job."

Hurt stared at the picture, He flipped it over and read the back, then tossed it onto the table. "You think this Masta did it?"

"Not sure. I know his address, but Vaypa T's goons made sure my line of inquiry came to an abrupt end this morning."

"You think you are well enough to go hunting tonight? I pulled three needles out of your back, set your arm, and bandaged the other one before your suit covered it up. You never told me: How did you make that suit?"

"Where did you get the beef?"

Captain Hurt smiled, revealing his uneven teeth. "A cow."

No Face grinned back. "Help me to my feet, you idiot. After I take a leak, I'll tell you the rest of the details on our way to Masta Mo's."

It was just past midnight by the time they reached Masta Mo's house. It was in a rundown portion of the city. A small wire fence surrounded the property. The grass had long since died, and whatever flecks of paint still clinging to the house were barely hanging on.

Hurt got out of the car and stretched. "I don't see why I couldn't have just leaped here."

"A super that can leap for kilos at a time would draw unnecessary attention to what we are doing."

"Suppose. You are certain the corporations are in on this somehow?"

It was strange hearing that word. He had completely forgotten about it, yet when Hurt used it, it was like being shaken awake from a dream. This word had been wiped from almost every dictionary and from every mind on the planet. Yet somehow, the man recalled it and used it.

"All signs point to it. The doll spying on Jenna's place mentioned it, as well as Vaypa."

"Great. The word of a junkie and a pimp."

"How do you remember these words?"

Hurt just shrugged, "Just lucky I guess." As they walked toward the house, he added, "Still not solid proof about corpor, er, Ad-Hoc involvement."

"It's a lead. If two separate people say something happened, you need to follow up on—" No Face pulled his pistols from his shoulder holsters.

Hurt tried to finish his sentence, "Follow up on… it?"

No Face nodded toward the house. "The front door."

Hurt followed No Face's gaze to the front of the house. The door showed no sign of forced entry, yet it was open an inch or two. Hurt wrapped his arm round No Face and leaped over the fence.

As they got closer to the door, they saw it was not forced, but some kind of corrosive had been used to dissolve the lock. He suspected they would not find Masta Mo amongst the living.

Passing the foyer, he found his suspicions were correct. The main living area had been gutted of furniture. Servers and other computer apparatuses were stacked around the room. Some were state-of-the art, some ancient relics from the dawn of the computer age. Regardless, everything had been smashed.

Masta Mo appeared to be a fence for stolen data. A data jock.

In the middle of the room was a gibbous-moon-shaped table. Three keyboards and five huge monitors stood monolith-like upon it. In a padded office chair sat Masta Mo. The front of his head rested on one of the keyboards, the back of it was missing. Clear fluid clouded with blood, the remains of his memories, ran down his back.

No Face motioned to Captain Hurt to search the rest of the area while he checked the computers. Hurt nodded and wandered into another room with a silence belaying someone of his size.

Inspecting the back of Mo's head, No Face saw it had been crushed by a heavy instrument. The wound looked like nothing he had seen before, some kind of new implant maybe?

No Face then maneuvered through the debris on the floor to the computer area. He was about to pull out his data cube, when he noticed the entire back of the machine had been torn out. The hard drive was missing.

Whatever this computer contained was taken or destroyed, or both. No Face assumed all the computers in the room were in the same condition. While he was unconscious, someone completely destroyed this trail.

He cursed himself for going to Vaypa's before coming here. Maybe Masta Mo would still be alive for questioning, and the data intact.

Or maybe someone was tying up loose ends and would have gotten there first, regardless. He kneeled to inspect Mo's shoes. They didn't match the work boot print he found next to the dumpster the night before. Oddly, they were classy dress shoes. Mo wore torn denims, a black t-shirt with a video game slogan, and fingerless gloves. Why the nice shoes? Most data jocks he knew dressed like an unmade bed.

He removed one of Mo's shoes. It was a size eight. Something was odd about it. Despite being faux-leather with a wooden sole, it seemed to weigh less that it should. He struck it a few times against the side of the metal frame of the desk. The third strike resulted in a crunching sound. The heel was tilted.

He grasped it and slid it off, revealing a small compartment hiding a data stick. He picked the stick up and loaded it into his PDA.

A video recording of Masta Mo began. Despite being a young man in his mid-twenties, he looked much older, as if he had not slept for months. He gasped heavily, as if he just ran a marathon.

"Hey sis. Suppose to get chow this week and yap about brateing moms and pops anniverse. But I am deep. You are too. I tried to scrub your dealings. But the Ad-Hocs know all. See all. I am sorry I brought you into this. Thought liftin' was easy scratch. But nothin' easy when 'Hocs are in play. End it with Jatta Jutta. She part of it, but not sure how. When you find this, take what scratch you have in savings and get far from here. Far as you can. Heart plus sis. Wish you glad times. Yo brah, Mo."

No Face held the PDA and rescanned what he just read, "They're brother and sister."

Hurt came back into the room holding a strange electronic device in an oversized hand. "Hmm?"

No Face handed the PDA to the other man who scanned the contents. "Jenna and Masta Mo were brother and sister. He introduced 'lifting' to her so she could earn some extra money."

"Who is Jatta Jutta and what's the connection?" Hurt said as he handed the PDA back.

"The Media Moguls have people on the streets generating the stories, who then send them to the nets. The newskickers then 'break' these stories on the visiscreens. Jatta Jutta is one of the more famous of these newskickers. My guess would be that she is also one of their clients."

"I haven't owned a visiscreen in ages. I'd rather spend my money elsewhere."

Hurt suddenly remembered the electronic device he had in his other hand and showed it to No Face. "Multitray."

"For downloading information from multiple sources at once. Usually to steal large amounts of information quickly. Highly illegal for non-Ad-Hocs."

Hurt handed the Multitray over to No Face, "Impossible to get for non-Ad-Hocs. Mo must be an exceptional thief, or…"

"Or he had some connection with them. Maybe even working for them. Think Jatta is involved?"

"Let's ask."

"You realize this will end up becoming violent."

"Didn't bring me along to win a beauty contest."

No Face suddenly remembered beauty contests, another memory he didn't know he had. But as they left, he noticed Captain Hurt brought the Multitray along with him.

⫘

Just before two o'clock, they parked a few blocks away from the BBS residence building. The Better Broadcasting System was owned by a conglomerate of some of the largest Ad-Hocs in the world. Therefore, it was one of the most watched. Any data on the newest vids, games, sports, and biz ran through it.

Once the Axiom AI system was hooked up to the internet, everything became monitored. Hence, everything that was not approved by the Ad-Hocs was shut down.

They got out of the car and looked up at the building.

No Face checked his gear and weapons, "You know they will have cameras on the roof as well."

"But less than on the ground. On the roof, they only have to worry about supers, and most of them are in their back pocket."

"Gotta point. You sure you can jump that far? That's at least a half of a kilo, maybe more."

Captain Hurt stared at the top of the building for a moment, gauging the distance. He shifted his gaze back to No Face and nodded, "No problem. I'd be more worried about losing your hat."

"It's specially made. It adheres to the suit unless I specifically give it a mental command to release." To prove his point, he took the hat from his head for an instant, then replaced it.

"Gotta tell me about that suit someday."
"I built it. It's made from a special carbon fiber that—"

Hurt wrapped his arm around No Face and crouched, judging the distance again. "Someday, not today. Got bad guys to catch." With one push of his powerful legs, he rocketed them both into the air.

Hurt skipped a few steps as they landed on the roof, before coming to a stop.

No Face hunched over placing his hands on his knees, "That was…"

Hurt brushed his unkempt hair out of his face, "Exhilarating? Exciting?"

"Nauseating. I think my stomach is still on the ground."

"Get used to it after a while."

"We need to hurry. I should be invisible to the cameras, but you won't be."

Hurt strode over to the door leading into the building and tore the door off its hinges.

"Once this job is done, remind me to teach you some lock picking skills. The idea is to not leave a trail."

"Point taken."

Footsteps echoed up the stairwell.

No Face made a 'told you so' gesture toward the stairs. His companion just shrugged and rolled his eyes. A guard charged up the stairs. Upon seeing the two intruders, he raised a cybernetic arm and let loose with a crackle of energy, striking Hurt in the chest and burning a good portion of his shirt away.

Hurt stood unaffected, like the Colossus of old.

The surprised guard shrieked, "Supers!"

The larger man propelled himself across the short distance. His fist connected with the guard's temple with such force, the metal skull under his skin dented as he fell to the floor.

"Th-th-that's all folks."

No Face tilted his head quizzically. "He's not dead. You merely knocked him unconscious."

"Never mind."

No Face shook his head in befuddlement as he retrieved a flat tablet from his pocket. He brought up a schematic of the building.

When he was sure they were on the correct path to Jatta's residence, he replaced the device and descended the stairs.

Hurt asked, "Why do you carry all that stuff? Wouldn't it be easier to be wired?" His tone was so casual that one would think he was taking a stroll in a park instead of breaking into the residence of one of the most popular media personalities of the BBS.

"Why aren't you wired?"

"Invulnerable skin. Can't get implants. Not even a residence chip."

"The more wired you are, the greater vulnerability you are to EMP charges. Not to mention, Nietzsche's quote about looking into the abyss. If you look in long enough, the abyss looks into you. And before you ask, I am chipped, but the suit covers the signal. Giving me full anonymity while wearing it."

"But isn't it—"

"You want to know this now?"

"Just thought of it now."

"You wouldn't let me tell the story when we were back on the ground, you will have to wait for an explanation."

They reached the fortieth floor and No Face slunk up to the door leading into the main hallway. Crouching, he opened it a sliver and peered through. He saw the desk of the guard they dispatched upstairs. A few feet away was the door to Jatta's residence, a potted plant on either side of the door.

"Can you get us in?"

No Face strode over to the door and knocked on it with a gloved fist. They heard the door unlock, indicating they can now enter.

"I'll question Jatta, you keep an eye on the door. Keep any guards who show up busy if they try to start anything. It's doubtful we will ever be able to convict her, even if she is the guilty party. But we owe it to Jenna to at least follow the trail to its very end."

The larger man nodded and clenched his fists.

As they slowly pushed the door open, it was like they entered another world. A thick ivory colored rug covered the center of the white marble floor. The walls were also ivory white. Various paintings in lively colors adorned the walls, looking like bright flowers along a background of summer clouds.

The leather chairs in the main living area a short distance away were solid black, heavily contrasting the walls and floors of the room. Even more starling was how clean everything was. The entire area seemed to have not seen a speck of dirt in its entire existence. A stark contrast to the world they knew.

A female voice came from a dark hallway, "Supers huh? Well, I have fans of all walks of life. How can I help you?"

Stepping into the light, Jatta was even more stunning in person than on visiscreen. Metallic purple lipstick sparkled on her full lips, and her green eyes still had the blue eyeliner from her latest broadcast.

She stood taller than No Face, though not quite as tall as Captain Hurt. Her long black hair reached all the way to her waist where it clung to the shapely curve of her left hip. A gold chain hung around her neck, the lower part of it disappearing under her shirt.

She wore an in-style slipsuit, a cross between elegant eveningwear and exercise leggings, yet cut so one could still go running in it. Made of bio-material, it probably cost more money than No Face would see in a decade.

No Face replied, "We are here to ask you a few questions."

"Oh?" She shifted her weight from one foot to the other. She moved like a panther, graceful yet deadly. She strode toward them. "I didn't know supers worked for the fan vids." She stopped directly in front of No Face, her lips just a few finger widths from his. "So, what can I help you with?"

No Face backed up a step and lied, "Married. Happily married."

Jatta appeared to have just bit into a raw lemon, then turned into a smile of someone who always got what she wanted. "What a horrible word. I didn't think people did such things these days." She turned to the other man. "And how about?"

"Just here to break stuff." Hurt said as he twisted one fist into another.

"Hmph," Jatta said as she stuck out her lower lip in a pouting gesture. "Well then, at least let a lady offer you something to drink while you ask your questions." She beckoned the two men to follow her further into her apartment. It felt like a noose being pulled about their necks.

"Where were you last night, around three AM?"

"Here, of course. I am sure you know that I have broadcasts at seven in the morning, again at noon, and again at seven in the evening. Doesn't give a good girl like me much time to wander the streets at night being bad." She led them into the living area. A lavish couch sat in front of a visiscreen that almost filled the entire wall. Nearby sat a desk made of real wood, dark in color. On it sat the latest in quanto-computing technology. Along the far wall sat a fully stocked bar, which was Jatta's destination. She pulled a bottle off the counter, then retrieved three glasses.

No Face held out a black gloved palm. "None for me. On duty."

She looked up at Hurt, who just continued to glower at her.

"Isn't the good cop, bad cop thing a bit dated?"

No Face realized the meaning of her words and looked over at his companion. "He's just like that." Looking back to Jatta. "This is pertaining to the murder of a Jenna Alhubru. She was found burned alive in a dumpster in the west side of the city." Jatta's face remained statue-like. Either she was a robot or she knew something. Few people remained emotionless upon hearing news of someone being burned alive.

"Tragic. The west end is a truly forsaken place. Surely you should be checking with slingers and angry love seekers, not me." She sipped her glass casually, yet methodically. Like she was weighing them up.

"That's the thing. Our trail led to love brokers—a 'slinger', as you so put it—named Vaypa."

Her face remained emotionless, but her eyes rapidly darted back and forth between the two men.

"Vaypa led us to Masta Mo, someone who deals with illegal data. And that trail led us directly to you."

"What use would I have for illegal data?"

"As a news reporter, there are plenty of reasons why illegal data would interest you. But I suspect something else."

She sipped her drink with a calculated look on her face.

"You see, when I was at Masta Mo's shop, three drones were waiting for me. They even confiscated some of the proof I found. What would the Axiom computer want with details of a simple murder investigation?"

Mentioning the A.I. that helped run the city changed Jatta's expression from cold calculation to worry. "Do not mention anything else! Do you know what the penalty is for treason against the state? It doesn't matter if you are supers or that I am a reporter, we will end up at the Truthseekers."

"Strange you bring that up, since all signs point to that you are selling the illegal data too. The drones were a bit of a tip off. But…"

She cut him off, "You have no proof nems. Now, why don't you and your dim lapdog get out of here? I have proof on camera that you are trespassing." She gestured at a camera peering from the ceiling, which wasn't there a few moments before. Turning her back to them, she poured another drink.

No Face stepped forward to grab the chain from around her neck and pulled it from beneath her gown. At the end was a golden heart, the chain looped through the piercing stud.

"We have photos of Jenn wearing this exact same stud before she was killed. Care to inform us how you came by it?"

For a second, the world stopped. Then, with speed so fast the human eye could barely follow, she spun around with a wine bottle in hand. She smashed No Face in the temple with it, punching him in the chest with equal speed. He flung across the room, colliding with the wall and slumping to the floor.

Before Jatta withdraw her arm, Hurt slammed into her. His fist colliding with her chin. She spiraled to the floor. To his surprise, she kicked her leg, and the momentum carried her back to her feet. She crouched and looked at her new target.

"Now I see why he brought you along. He's the brains, you're the muscle."

"I'm the whole package."

"Cocky. I like that." She picked up a nearby chair and launched it at her opponent. Hurt raised his hand to shield his face instinctively. It shattered against his forearm like a wave striking a rocky shore. The gesture took his eyes from his opponent long enough to let Jatta renew her attack. She grasped his upraised arm then used her knee to place two swift knee strikes into his stomach.

As Hurt reeled from the blows, she punched his windpipe, knocking him to his knees. As he fell, she continued raining blows onto the back of his head, determined to put the larger man down for the count.

He brought his fist down on her left foot so hard it cracked the floor beneath it. She yowled in pain. He tried to regain his feet as she managed a few more blows, despite trying to avoid putting weight on her left leg.

As Hurt regained his feet, "You're a cyborg or a super?"

She screamed at him in anger and struck him again, this time right between the eyes. As his head snapped back, she followed up with a solid punch to his groin. Then repeated the strike three more times.

Preoccupied with punching him in his crotch, she could not dodge in time as two oversized hands grasped her by the shoulders. She glanced up as Hurt's face collided with hers, crushing her nose. A fountain of blood spattered across her lips, chin, cleavage, and the exposed golden heart.

She slumped to the floor.

"A Jeen. Borg would have a metal skull for all the wiring."

No Face walked up holding a coat and a pair of shoes. "You alright? Saw you had the situation under control, so I did some snooping while you two were dancing around."

"Invulnerable." He pointed at the unconscious form on the floor. "She's a Jeen."

"Genetically modified, huh? Makes sense. Only the extremely wealthy could afford that." He handed the articles of clothing to Hurt. "That would explain a lot. Those shoes were made at Masta Mo's. Recognize the stitching. I'd stake my suit on it. Size twelve and the treads match with the digicast I made the other night."

Captain Hurt just shrugged.

"Jatta wore the shoes, and most likely another form of disguise, so she could meet Jenna, murder her and burn the evidence."

No Face took out special handcuffs, strong enough for supers, rolled Jatta onto her stomach and placed them on her. "I will bet once we get her downtown, then search this place, we will find piles of illegal data on her computer."

"Leave this place alone? Doesn't seem wise."

"I thought of that as well. If she wakes up, I won't be able to handle her without you. Not to mention, you are not deputized, so you cannot make the arrest."

"Don't like it."

"Neither do I. But the law is the law. We got her now on attacking a deputized officer. Plus, with what you have in your hands and the fact she was in possession of Jenna's heart piercing, we can place her at the scene of the murder as well as being one of the last people to see Jenna alive. With that, we have enough cause to come back and search the place thoroughly.

"Still stinks."

"Pick her up. We need to get her to the car."

As they stepped out of the elevator on the ground floor, building security were waiting for them. "Hold it right there, No Face! We will take Jatta. You are kidnapping a BBS employee."

"Not at all. She is the primary suspect in the murder of Jenna Alhubru. We have proof she was at the scene of the murder and need to take her in for questioning."

"BBS law supersedes city law. We won't ask you again. Give us Jatta and leave. Last warning."

"Sorry. Under section 147 of the BBS code, murder suspects must be released to the city."

"That is for other BBS employees. Not some dirty nem."

"The code doesn't specify that."

The security forces glanced at each other. "Okay. But she is not allowed to speak to you unless a certified BBS legal team is there."

"Agreed."

"Agreed." The security officer pressed his temple to activate the broadcasting device in his head. "Let them though. Scramble legal to the station office. We need them there within fifteen minutes."

No Face walked past them with his hands in his coat pockets, as if casually strolling through the park. He headed to the door and left the building, Hurt and the unconscious Jatta in tow.

Hurt felt Jatta stir in his arms. Tears trickled down her cheek. She coughed, "Loved her."

No Face turned to look at her as they walked. "Hmm?"

She reached out with her hand and placed the golden heart piercing into his gloved hand. "Loved Jenna. But I had to. Becau—"

They hadn't made it thirty paces out of the building when a red beam struck Jatta in the head, slicing it in two.

Startled, the two men looked up and saw several Axidrones hovering in the air, waiting for the two men to make their next move. Multiple red dots appeared on No Face's heart and forehead.

The security officer's voice rung out from a nearby loudspeaker. "Again. Drop Jatta's remains on the ground. Then turn around and leave."

"And ignore the fact you murdered her?"

"She is —was a BBS employee on BBS property, in the process of giving up company secrets, thus a valid and legal target for silencing."

No Face and Hurt looked at each other. The former nodded toward the ground and the latter dropped the body, as one would drop a bag of garbage off on the curb.

Hurt glared at the drones, the building, and the security personnel. He clenched his fists and took a step back toward the building.

The security officer spoke up again. "If your next move is not turning around and leaving, you will have to scrape what's left of your friend off the ground with a sponge."

No Face reached out and placed his hand on the larger man's wrist, lowering it like one would to someone clutching a loaded weapon. "Let's go. It's not worth it." He looked down at the golden object is his hand. "The end of a dream. Jenna Alhubru will know peace at least."

The brutish man sighed and unclenched his hands. "Yeah."

As they turned to walk away, the Axidrones removed their targeting beams from No Face but silently watched the two men leave. The Uncovered Man swore that one day; they would pay the ultimate price.

STORY SEVEN

Winter's Burning Hearth

Heavy snowfall blurred the road and the attackers on it. The Covered Man swerved as the armor plated jeep tried to sideswipe the black car. The jeep could not gain traction on the snow and missed by inches. As it skidded by, he glimpsed the driver: A feline face covered with orange fur, a red bandana adoring its head.

Mutants.

As the Covered Man's attention focused on the jeep whizzing past, a second vehicle pulled alongside and two mutants to leaped onto his hood. One looked like a parrot with the mouth of a leech. It used its talons to dig into the metal of the hood.

The second appeared to be a naked human male except for the gray-green tentacle growing out of a hump on his back. As it landed on passenger side, it pressed its bare feet against the window and slapped the tentacle across the hood of the car, its suction cups holding it in place.

Switching his focus, the Covered man drew his pistol and fired several shots into the chest of the naked human. Pain flashed across his face for a moment, then it twisted into a smile full of black crooked teeth.

As it climbed through the window, the parrot-thing on the hood clawed a large hole in the roof of the vehicle.

The Covered Man punched his foot to the floor and the black car pulled away from the other two vehicles as they turned around. He pumped more shots into the naked human, one cracking his jaw, the next piercing his left eye. He went limp, half stuck in the window.

He fired through the hole in the roof at the parrot-thing but it let go with one talon to bend backward, avoiding the round. It began clawing at the roof again, tearing another piece from off large enough to allow it to enter the black car.

As flurries of snow whipped past, it bent itself in half to press its face against the hole. Long tendrils wove from its mouth, grasping at the Covered Man's head.

He pulled his foot from the gas and pushed himself upward to grab the throat of the parrot-thing. The tendrils wrapped around his goggles.

The parrot thing's legs snapped as the Covered Man muscles tensed, and he dragged the mutant through the hole, the jagged edges of metal shredding feathers and the flesh underneath. The thing let out a long and horrible screech as it flailed out at its assailant.

The Covered Man slammed the thing's head into the dashboard again and again until its head cracked. He shoved it into the passenger seat next to the bleeding naked human.

Before the Covered Man could grab the wheel, the black car lurched as one of his pursuers slammed into him. His forehead struck the steering wheel, driving his goggles into his face.

Trying to shake the cobwebs from his mind, he pushed his foot back onto the gas pedal. Tires spun on the slick road, causing the car to slide sideways onto the shoulder, its back end now firmly lodged in a snowbank in the ditch.

The two cars sped past. The Covered Man frantically searched for his pistol, but it must have fallen to the floor in the rear-end collision. The two cars were slowing down to circle back for the kill. He had to think fast.

Getting out of the car, he stood with door open next to his vehicle, placing himself between his attacker and the black car. As they finished their turn, once again revving their engines, one pulled a bit in front of the other.

As the car raced forward, ready to crush the life from both man and machine, the Covered Man reached into his vehicle and retrieved the corpse of the parrot-thing. Using every bit of his strength, he hurtled it into the windshield of the approaching car.

The car attempted to swerve, but the dead body struck the windshield. It clipped the front of the black car before careening off the opposite side of the road.

The armored jeep slammed on its brakes, skidding in the snow. The Covered Man pulled the tentacled, naked human from the car, ready to launch this corpse just like the last as soon as it came within range.

Seconds ticked by. As they faced each other, they gauged weak spots and the others' strength. The armored jeep spun its tires in the snow and raced off back east, towards Mad Town.

The Covered Man watched the car speed away for a moment, making sure it would not return for another attack. He dropped the dead, human-looking mutant on the road. Reaching back into the car, he retrieved his pistol and snapped a new clip into it.

Raising a hand to shield his eyes from the falling snow, he trudged through the bad weather looking where the other vehicle went into the ditch.

The car was there, its front end half sunk into a pond. A figure, blurred by the weather, stumbled through the snow. It was hunched over and kept its right arm hugged tight against its stomach.

The Covered Man caught up to his prey easily. The mutant appeared like a fox with pointed ears and a narrow muzzle. It had a heavy gash, still oozing blood, along its side.

The mutant spoke a crude form of English, mixed in with wheezes and guttural animal sounds, half-shouting so it could be heard over the wind. "You reek of the Hairless. Beast is coming. Beast leads the Chosen. Beast will feed. We will wipe your remains from—"

A hammer-like fist struck the mutant in the side of the head. A spattering of blood stained the snow.

≻ᴠᴠ≺

By the time the black car reached the outskirts of Blac Arth, the falling snow reduced visibility to just a few feet. The Covered Man had to honk the horn to get those stationed on the wall to notice him. Rolling through, he turned on the next road to the original wall the seven pioneers of Blac Arth built months ago.

At the end of the street lay The Shop. Before the snows fell, the settlers claimed and fixed up the connecting building to the south of the Shop and made it into an armory and prison. Between the walled-off Box, the firehouse, and both parts of The Shop, the residents of the Settlement had managed to repel numerous attackers over the past months.

The numbers of the settlement also grew. They were over a hundred. Families from all over had come. Like water pulled down a drain, a sliver of the BeforeTimes captivated the imaginations and hopes of many.

He passed the small cemetery they erected in the area west of The Box and north of The Shop. It overlooked the creek, and served for the time being. There were plans to reclaim the old cemetery to the northeast next summer, but they didn't have the materials or manpower to expand that far yet.

There were already a few graves there. Bodok, who was burned to death by a firebomb. Innie, who was speared in the head by a raider. And of course, the original resident, who was known only as 'Nameless Mother'.

Stopping in front of SouthShop, as it became known, he stepped out of the car. Even with his goggles, he had to raise a hand to block the wind and snow so he could see where he was going.

Heading to the trunk, he opened it, revealing its passenger. Bound with iron cable and a cloth wrapped around its head, the mutant shrieked at him and strained at his bonds. As the Covered man picked up the mutant, it tried to bite him. Between the cloth around its head and the material of his suit, its attack met with failure.

He hoisted the living bundle over his shoulder and then slammed the trunk shut. Approaching the building, his boots crunched in the newly fallen snow. Immediately inside the door stood Sike, Javier, and another settler he didn't recognize. The first two had their guns at the ready. Upon seeing the Covered Man, they let out a relieved sigh and Sike hung his pistol back in the holster on his hip.

Javier asked, "How's hunting?"

The Covered Man turned so they could see the hooded figure slung over his shoulder. "Survivor. Need answers."

Sike nodded and walked down the hallway, removing a ring of keys from his belt.

The settler that the Covered Man didn't recognize spoke. "The mutants are out in weather like this? Unbelievable."

Sike said, "My ancestors, the Waaswaaganiwininiwag, hunted the lands far north of here without the benefits of technology."

Javier grinned at his friend's stoic nature. Slapping the Covered Man on his free shoulder, he asked, "How about it, big guy? Since the storm hit, you think mutants will really attack?"

"Two vehicles. One escaped. Doing something. Not making snowmen."

Sike led the others into a large room with walls made of concrete. Three makeshift cells sat alongside one of the walls, all empty.

The brutish figure strode into the nearest cell. Javier pointed his pistol at the mutant's head. Sike stood by, ready to shut the door to the cell, key ready in the lock.

As the Covered Man set the living bundle on the floor, it began frantically kicking and spasming, desperately trying to free itself. A large black boot struck it in the head, and it lay still once more.

The settler the Covered Man didn't recognize said, "You don't have to treat it so rough! It's a living thing."

Javier shook his head, "Kid, mutants are evil through and through."

Removing the cloth from its head. The youth audibly gasped, seeing what lay beneath. Its head looked like a fox with a tinge of humanity wrapped up in a cloak of madness. He backed up a step.

Javier glanced in his direction but kept the pistol fixed on the thing on the floor. "Now you see what we are up against. They want to see us on a dinner plate, or extinct. Or both."

"But, where did they come from?"

The Covered Man grabbed the mutant by the scruff of the neck and dragged it to a sitting position against the concrete wall of the cell. While removing the bonds from its legs, he left those around its arms. "Humans. Thought they could beat the odds. Genetics had the last laugh."

He left the cell, and in one swift moment, locked the door, and tossed the keys to Sike, who hung them on his belt.

The Covered Man turned to the youth, "Mutants hate hairless."

"Hairless?"

"Their name for us."

"Why? I haven't done anything to it."

The Covered Man grabbed the youth and lowered his face so his goggles were mere inches from the other's face. "Dinner done anything to you before eating? The raiders burning and killing care what you have done? Raiders don't put your intestines out and eat them as you watch."

The youth's eyes went as wide as saucers and lip trembled. He tried to say something, but only stammered.

Sike said, "Monnic, why don't you run next door and tell Joshua about our prisoner? Or your way back, guard the front door again."

Monnic ran back to the front door, looking back once, unsure of who was more monstrous in the room.

Javier ran his free hand through his hair, trying not to laugh. "Outside is summertime compared to how cold you are."

Sike interrupted. "Enough jokes, where did you find our friend?"

"Bout halfway through here and CroPlay. Vehicle crashed. Salmon pond."

"Joshua will want to hear of this. More and more mutants becoming mobile can't be good."

Javier said, "I have never even heard of mutants driving before. Have you, big guy?"

The Covered Man nodded. "Yeah. Rare until now."

The Fox thing regained some composure and fixed its beady eyes on the three men on the other side of the metal bars that now surrounded it. It launched itself at the bars, slamming into them, reopening the wound on its muzzle.

"Meat! Hairless food! Smell your fear. Pack is running. Lead by Big Beast! Tender hairless flesh will feed so the Pack can grow."

The Covered Man strode forward to the bars. The mutant cowered from his captive.

"Even you. Think your different? No. All will end up in the gullet. The Pack will grow. Oh yes it wi—*ulk!*"

The Covered Man reached up through the metal bars and grabbed the rambling, crazed thing by the throat. Pulling it toward him so it smashed its face on the bars.

"Why out in the storm?"

"Food. Looking for stragglers, tasty like those behind you."

With another flex of his arm, the mutant struck its head against the metal bars.

"Why?"

"Ahh! Hate you hairless! *Hate!*"

With another head strike against the bars, its muzzle leaked from both nostrils and its right eye swelled shut.

"Argh! We building! Building the grand! Unlike the hairless that cracked the world and the skies above, the Chosen Ones will save the planet! Failed species! Failed System! The Pack will bring peace everywhere!"

Javier mumbled, "By eating everyone that opposes you."

"Building what?"

"The Grand! That which will put you into memory!"

"Grand? Grand what?"

"Big Beast knows! The Chosen knows!" It stopped and shot a sly look at the Covered Man and continued in a lower voice. "One of you hairless knows."

Joshua's voice came from behind them. "What? One of us?"

The Covered Man looked back at them. Joshua and Rays stood there, flecks of melting snow coated their hair and shoulders. Turning back to the mutant he held tight, he asked, "Who?"

The thing laughed, sounding like a cross between a high pitched human laugh and a beastial cackle that sent a shiver down the spine of the non-supers in the room.

The Covered Man tightened his fist around its neck. The laugher became strained as he squeezed its windpipe, but it didn't slow down at all.

With a shove, he sent the thing against the far concrete wall. Hacks and coughs mixed in with its endless cackling as the wind was knocked out of it.

Javier shook his head. "A spy? In Blac Arth? Unlikely, that thing is just crazy."

Rays nodded. "Anyone out in this weather has to be. Right, Trash Bag?"

Joshua grimaced. "We can't take the chance. We need to shift some people from snow removal to making ammo. Shift some power from heat to the lights on the walls."

Javier shook his head, "If we do that, people will freeze!"

Joshua replied, "What would you have me do? If the spy exists and these things get the jump on us, none of us will survive to see spring."

"Need to scout."

Joshua said, "Want any of us to come with you?"

"No. Preparations." He turned and looked at Rays. "Anyone at Shop?"

Rays just smiled. "Why yes! Kristine is there. She will be happy to see you."

"Hhhh." The Covered Man said as he moved through them to the door.

⋟⋞

He had only been inside for fifteen minutes and the black car was already covered in snow. Using his hand as a scraper, he began brushing the accumulation to the ground.

His mind wandered to a time long ago, when he barely could look over the hood of the car. When each family lived in their own house. Friends and family would stand outside the door and sing songs. They would be invited in for food and drink. Everyone laughed.

Like snowflakes that were things of beauty, they drifted through the air without a care in the world. But the moment they landed on him, they melted and disappeared.

Lost.

With goggled eyes, he stared up into the infinite white flakes that fell upon him. Each like a screaming voice from his past. He again questioned the wisdom of staying here.

The settlement grew day by day. Surely, he didn't have to stay. Why did he? For some vague hope that those memories could be pulled to the present and rebuilt? Even if that was true, wouldn't everyone be better off if he reverted to his nomadic ways?

Sike. Linda. Javier. David. All of them treated him as one of the group. Like his allies of old. But they had no clue about his past. Rays treated him like a brother.

And Kristine. He saw the way she looked at him, all the more after the Raider attack a few months ago when he and Rays found her in the southern ruins of Blac Arth. But she could never be allowed to see what was underneath. Not just under the suit, but who he was at his core, and what he did.

He got in the car and drove it the twenty feet necessary to reach the doors of The Shop. He lifted the large garage door and moved the car inside. Kristine was there, cleaning and oiling her rifle.

Her sharpshooting abilities had surpassed Linda's by far over the past few months. Maybe even as good as Manny.

Her face lit up when she saw him. Setting down the rifle, she stood up and strode over to him.

The Covered Man took the gas handle from the pump and began to refuel. With the settler's ingenuity, they now created their own gasoline. It acted like a gas station of old. Fuel on demand. But it was like everything else here. An illusion. He felt the open road pull at him. To leave everyone here to make their own way against the mutants. Once again, he stayed.

"Dad said you captured a mutant!"

He simply nodded as he checked he went through his ammo pouches.

"Scary. Did you make it talk? Why are they attacking us?"

"Just nonsense. Almost as crazy as Babblers." Babblers were once humans that went insane from cannibalism and living off scraps of the BeforeTimes. Mutants were genetically altered to be what they were.

Kristine watched as he counted out twelve shells for the pipe sawed-off he now carried. Rays built it for him a month or so ago. He grabbed two clips for the P-10 pistol. It was a made before the collapse, so it jammed once in a while, but it would suffice until he found something better. Before he left, he made sure he had the full capacity of three grenades on his belt.

"Where are you going now?"

"East."

"Hunting more mutants?"

He made no reply as he removed the gas nozzle and hung it back up on the pump.

As he turned around, Kristine was right there. She took a step closer, so her body pressed right up against his. "You have been patrolling a lot these days. Why don't you let me come with you? After the incident in the south a few months back, you should know I can hold my own." Kristine waited, and when no reply came, she hoped that was a sign he would let her go with him. She trotted back to the table and began to reassemble the rifle as fast as she could.

The Covered Man climbed into the car. Before shutting the door, he said, "Close the door when I'm gone." The black car revved to life.

"No! Take me with you!" Kristine hastened her rifle assembly. "You need someone to watch your back!"

He backed the black car out and turned it around, then disappeared into the blizzard before it reached the end of the street.

The black car moved at a snail's paces down the highway. The visibility had gotten worse. The Covered Man barely recognized the battlefield from earlier that day. It was completely snowed over. He breathed a sigh of relief when he reached the outskirts of CroPlay. At least he had signs and buildings to mark where the edges of the road were.

A few bundled up figures gave chase on foot. Whether they were raiders, mutants, or babblers didn't matter. He soon left them far behind in the rear-view mirror.

It was early afternoon when the forest and fields switched to ruined shells of buildings, marking that he was approaching the outskirts of Madtown.

The snow let up, allowing the Covered Man to see further than just a few dozen feet. He felt uneasy as he drove on, having never gotten this close to MadTown before. He never thought he would be this close. The hair on the back of his neck stood on end.

He saw the overpass for the old Highway 12 ahead. The right side had collapsed, with other debris piled on top of it, making it an effective blockade. Between the sections of the highway above stood a makeshift gate. On the wall above, protected from the wind, large fires blazed. It cast ominous shadows on the stone columns and slopes beneath.

The Covered Man slowed the car to a stop about fifty yards from the overpass, in an ancient T-intersection. In this storm, there were unlikely few on the prowl, but he kept the car moving as quiet as possible. Snow raced past the windshield. He glanced about. There was no one to be seen.

He wondered about turning around and heading back, but his stubbornness got the better of him. He could not go back empty handed. Should he turn around and go hide out in a building, hoping a patrol would happen by? Or should he attempt the open the gate?

Again, his single-mindedness got the better of him. He would creep up to the gate and see if he heard anyone. If not, he would check to see if the gate could be opened.

Getting out of the car, he made a last check of his gear before closing the door as slow as could be so it didn't make any noise. The howling wind and the soft crunch of the snow underfoot were drowned out by the heavy thumping of his heart. No one actively went looking for mutants, and here he was, sneaking up to a settlement of them.

The snow lessened as the overpass ahead shielded him from the weather. The gate itself was an impressive thing: A truck trailer with multiple iron spikes pounded through it. Rusty barbed wire decorated the top like tinsel on a Christmas tree.

He formulated a plan on how to get around it and took a step forward.

A rifle shot rang out, catching him in the chest. The force spun him around to land face first in the snow.

Someone yelled, "Damn. You are one tough owl." It was Fappa Jack. "Hit him again!"

His head pounded from the pain and his vision blurred, but he knew he had to get off the road. Another shot rang out just as propelled himself a few feet off the road and into the ditch on the north side. The second bullet grazed his right shoulder.

Rolling over once to get further into the ditch, he left a trail of crimson.

Out of sight of the gate, he could still hear Jack shouting. "Get out there! He's still alive. Hunt him down! I'll make sure he cannot escape."

A burble of inhuman voices cackled and murmured as the gate opened with a slow groan of metal.

The Covered Man rolled onto his side and pushed himself up. He had to make it to the car. They were ready for him. If all the mutants were this organized under Jack, they would sweep over Blac Arth like a hurricane washing away a sandcastle.

Pushing himself to a half standing position, he felt like he was going to vomit. A dog headed mutant ran across the road holding a sniper rifle. It stopped a few feet away and pulled out a pistol with its free hand.

Clenching his fist tight around a handful of snow, he flung the crude snowball at the mutant. It instinctively ducked. When it recovered, the Covered Man had a pistol in hand and emptied the clip into it, only hitting it three of the seven shots. But it was enough to drop it to the road.

It dropped its pistol nearby in the snow, and clamored to retrieve it, its clawed hand searching erratically. The Covered Man stood up and sprinted toward his car.

The crack of the sniper rifle tore through the snowy air. No pain? It must have missed. The Covered Man stumbled forward before he caught himself, still dazed from the wounds in his chest and shoulder.

Straining to focus, he heard shouts coming from behind him, muffled by the falling snow. But it didn't matter; he was a mere few steps from the black car, and he could escape to warn Blac Arth Fappa Jack was now in league with the mutants of MadTown and make plans on how to deal with him.

As he grasped the door handle, a loud whoosh came from the direction of the gate. A rocket screamed across the sky like a low-flying plane, directly at him.

The Covered Man had enough time to let go of the handle and turn to run before it struck the black car directly in the hood. The violent explosion enveloped both him and the vehicle.

He was flung into the air like a rag doll, flipping head over heels into space. He landed in the snow and skidded to a stop. Pieces of debris flung through the air like fiery flakes of metallic snow.

The victorious screams of mutants weaved through the storm. He knew he had to get up. His head pounded even worse and his body felt like one big bruise. Thinking back to the days bullets bounced off of him, he missed them.

The Covered Man tried to stand. He wanted to vomit. He raised his head to see where his pursuers were. The burning wreckage of his car lay about fifty feet away. The burning remains would draw the mutants right to it. Despite the pain and unsteadiness, he got to his feet.

He turned his back on the burning wreckage and moved as fast as he could. He couldn't sprint; his bodily injuries prevented it.

Clutching a hand to the chest wound to attempt to hold in enough blood to survive this, he pushed himself to move faster. Hopefully, he still had enough of his regeneration ability remaining to save him.

To his left, ruined buildings were discernible through the falling snow, so he decided to make for them. While his suit masked his heat and scent, the mutant's animalistic tracking ability would spot his footprints long before the snow hid them.

Fappa Jack's voice was barely audible through the storm, "Run, Owl! Run!" If he said anything else, it was covered by the wind. This was followed by the guttural howls and growls on the mutants.

Another voice rolled over the snow, more inhuman than even the rest of the mutants. "Found you! No prey escapes Big Beast!" This was followed by a strange cacophony of mutant's howls, chirps, and roars. They picked up his trail.

He moved his legs like pistons to get to the ruined buildings, hoping they could provide him with cover. His feet struck something solid. An old parking lot, blanketed with snow, lay cracked and broken from ages of ill-repair. The world swirled and tilted from his head wound.

He lost his balance and pitched forward, getting a face full of snow as he struck the ground.

Pushing himself to his feet, he reached the first outcropping of buildings. They appeared to be restaurants of ages past. He rounded a corner of one and pressed his back up flat against it, attempting to catch his breath. The hum of engines approached. Through his goggles, he scanned the area, hoping an idea will present itself for his salvation.

Instead, a humanoid covered head to toe in shaggy fur came around the corner of the building. Its wolf-like head stared at him through yellow eyes. It crouched, ready for combat, and inhaled to cry to the others.

The Covered Man's hands closed around its head like a Venus flytrap. One hand clutched its skull while the other gripped its jaw. With a powerful twist, he tore its mandible halfway from its head.

It fell to the ground clutching at its ruined face, unable to make a sound louder than a gurgle.

The Covered Man ran to the largest building nearby, a super store from the BeforeTimes. One of the loading bays was open, the door torn off and laying in the snow nearby.

An acidic smell hung in the air as he leaped into the interior. It was dark, causing his goggles to kick in. "Charge: 100%," read out on the display. He reminded himself to thank Rays once he got back to Blac Arth. If he ever got back.

The mutants could not follow footprints in the snow where there was no snow. He could sneak out a side door, and the heavy snow would cover his tracks. At the very least, the delay in the chase would allow his the pain in his temple to reside.

Most places were heavily looted as the world collapsed, but this place had been stripped bare. Some of the rows of metallic shelves lining the center of the room were missing as well. Once used to stock things for the masses to buy, they were gone. Along with the money. Along with the masses.

The smell of acid increased, and he spotted one of the metallic shelves, half dissolved as if a giant had swallowed it and spit it back out still coated with stomach juices. Nearby, a few bones of rats or rat-like things hissed and popped as the same powerful acid broke them down into a puddle even as he watched.

He drew his pistol, reloaded it, and checked his grenades. If what he suspected was here, he was in deep trouble. Facing off against fifty hostile mutants didn't seem as dangerous. He slowed his pace and tried to move as quiet as he could.

Multiple shouts echoed from out in the storm. They found the wolf-headed mutant. The footprints in the snow would lead them inside.

Advancing further into the interior, he looked for any exits he could, paying close attention to any holes in the floor, despite how small, careful to avoid them.

Passing a small employee area, he headed out into the main area of the store. A large path had been burned through the piles of empty boxes, demolished furniture, and broken palettes. This confirmed his fears. Seeing the area mostly filled with clutter gave him hope it would be too busy to deal with him.

He moved along the left wall, away from the path. Once he reached the corner, he would be near the wall facing Blac Arth. Trying a door farther away would be wiser, since it would increase the time it would take the mutants to find his trail, but that changed.

Picking his way through the debris, a section of old grills and outdoor cooking supplies, the Covered Man made his way along the wall as quiet as he could. From behind him, the feral voices of the mutants echoed off the walls, indicating they had entered the stores loading area.

Something shifted in the middle of the store. Something big.

The Covered Man quickened his pace, frantically searching for an exit. Any exit.

"Know you're here Shadowskin! Followed your trail!" The mutants had entered the main store area behind him. With the amount of noise they were making, he knew he was doomed. They all were.

One of the mutants spoke in their language made up of snarls, growls, chirps, and clicks. He spotted at least a dozen of them starting to search the area, probably more were searching the back.

They struck at the piles of garbage with makeshift clubs, axes, and swords in an attempt to find him or flush him out. Some of the mutants stood nearby with crudely made guns, prepared to open fire at whatever they found.

Two large grills piled on top of one another stood at the end of the row. The Covered Man crouched behind them and waited.

A group of five mutants headed in his direction - A horse with some kind of tumor over its left eye that wielded a hooked axe, something that looked like an armadillo, and two dog headed mutants, covered with fur. The last mutant was humanoid with a snake head, and its left arm was also a snake.

There was no way he could take them all out silently, even if his chest and shoulder didn't ache so much.

He changed his plan. Maybe he could take out these five and then make a break back to the loading dock door. Hopefully, there weren't more waiting and he could get past the rest of them.

The snake headed mutant used its snake arm to point directly at the Covered Man. "There!"

Five sets of eyes locked on him. Voices of mutants elsewhere in the building shrieked and jabbered in victorious sounds. He prepared to fight his way to freedom.

The screams of victory turned into screams of terror.

A huge mass of protoplasm about ten feet high erupted from the debris in the room. Massive pseudo-pods emerged from it. Everything it touched, whether wreckage or mutant, stuck to it fast, slowly being pulled inside of it.

Five of the mutants were instantly snatched up, and their howls of pain echoed off the walls as they were slowly absorbed. The two dog mutants ran to help their friends.

Gunfire rang out. As the bullets permeated its outer membrane, they just stopped and floated for a moment before being dissolved.

Just as he feared, a MHETooze. Genetically created for devouring plastics in the BeforeTime, they quickly evolved to feed on all sorts of garbage, including living things. They grew out of control after the Collapse, and now they intended to feed on everything.

Tumor-eyed horse, armadillo, and snake arm move to surround the Covered Man, hoping that their allies could hold of the MHETooze. They had no idea what they were dealing with; that thing would make short work of all of them.

Snake arm lashed out, attempting to sink both sets of fangs into him. The Covered Man lunged aside and drew the combat knife from his belt. In one fluid move, he severed the snake head arm at the elbow.

A well-placed kick to the stomach of the armadillo sent it reeling backwards, causing it to trip over some boxes and tumble to the floor.

The horse swung its axe in a downward arc. the Covered Man drove his blade deep where the arm and torso met, severing nerves and arteries alike. His free hand connected with the horse's non-tumorous eye, shattering it with a sickening sound.

A heap of nearby junk erupted, hurtling BeforeTime trash in every direction. A pseudopod rose into the air for an instant, only to strike the tumorous horse. Its neighing, human-like scream was soon silenced as the substance flowed over its head, dissolving flesh as it went.

In an instant, the Covered Man rethought his plan. He sheathed his knife and turned back toward the loading dock. Running directly at the remaining mutants who had formed a half circle around the mass and the air was riddled with screams and gunfire.

As he raced toward them, a mutant with an oversized shark's head and wielding a combat rifle fired burst after burst into the living mound with no effect. It turned and looked at him in surprise. The Covered Man struck his fist into the shark's jaw and used his other hand to slam a grenade into its mouth.

He could hear the screams of the armadillo and the snake headed mutants behind him as he pulled the rifle from the shark's grip. He put a boot to the shark, propelling it toward the mass, which promptly engulfed it.

The Covered Man tried to put as much distance between himself and the mass.

The following explosion caused the MHETooze to spread apart in a nebula-like pattern, parts of it reaching almost to the ceiling for an instant before it pulled itself back together.

Not waiting to see if it reformed, the Covered Man used the butt of the rifle to strike another cat-like mutant in the side of the head, then ran toward the exit.

As he rounded the corner to the docks, three more mutants stood there with guns at the ready. The combat rifle spit its metal death into the nearest, sending it crumbling to the floor.

The remaining two raised their weapons, their focus on something behind the Covered Man, then turned to jump off the loading dock and back out into the storm. Sounds of shelves behind toppled behind him, made him pick up the pace.

As he launched himself from the loading dock, he landed directly on one of the mutants, throwing it to the ground with him landing squarely on its back.

Before the other could react, the Covered Man unloaded the rest of his clip into it and turned around to run back toward the building. This time, however, he swerved to the left, carrying him along the outside of the structure. The ooze erupted from the loading dock, flowing over the two mutants.

The Covered Man kept running alongside the building, and did not slow down until he put plenty of distance between himself and the store.

As he stopped to catch his breath, he thought of his lost car and weapons. He needed to hurry back to Blac Arth. If Jack had been teaching the residents of Madtown about mechanics and technology, everyone there was in danger.

⟫≋⟪

Pushing forward through the falling snow, the Covered Man turned north and trudged through a long abandoned business park. The windows, glass long gone, stared at him with envy.

Within the hour, he reached The Thin Path. It went parallel to 'the 14', but a few miles north. It was named from the fact most of the blacktop and concrete that made up the road was gone. The majority of it was overgrown, and only a thin jagged line remained of the previous road upon which to walk.

He turned west to Blac Arth and began walking. About that time, the business park switched to suburban homes and the sun set. The weather didn't let up one bit and the Covered Man occasionally had to clear his weapons of snow. He counted his blessings it was not ice or sleet. If that built up on his gear, it would have been a lot harder to clear away.

He passed by odd-shaped lumps in the snow. Most likely old vehicles or large appliances torn from the houses they once dwelled in during the looting after the Collapse.

Soon, even the suburbs gave way to forests and long abandoned fields. The eerie, rhythmic creaking of trees came from a copse along the left side of the path, shaking in the wind enough that small fistfuls of snow tumbled from the branches.

As he passed by, he heard the distinct hoot of an owl. He drew his pistol and pointed it at the trees. Owls hunt more before storms, but hunker down during a storm. Whatever he heard was no owl.

He could feel something in that group of trees watching him. The only thing he could see with his goggles looked like a ten foot mound of snow.

214

While facing whatever it was, he began walking, periodically checking where he was going to make sure he didn't run into something. As he began to walk past it, he felt whatever lurked in those trees was tense. It knew its meal was aware of its presence and was now escaping.

A voice of a young girl came from the shape. "Help me. I am so hungry."

The Covered Man edged away, keeping his gun pointed at the shape.

"Why won't you help me?"

The shape shuffled, losing patience. More clumps of snow fell from trees as the thing bumped into them.

Two red eyes with no pupils, almost as tall as he was, opened in the mound as it got taller.

The little girl spoke again, this time infused with anger. "Why won't you help me?"

The Covered Man turned and ran. His legs pistoned through the heavy snow blanketing the ground, and he ran until his breath came in great gasps. Looking behind him, all he saw were large flakes of snow, and fields on both sides of the road. The windblown snow spiraled in the air, already filling in his footprints.

No sign of the mound or the red eyes. He looked again. Nothing. Did he really see anything? He was not so certain now.
He checked his wounds. Both had stopped bleeding at least. He would have to get medical treatment once he made his way back to Blac Arth.

He returned to his trek westward. At regular intervals, he glanced over his shoulder to make sure nothing followed.

When ruined houses covered with snow appeared again, he picked up his pace. The ruins of CroPlay were near. A small playground emerged from the darkness and falling snow covered the right side of the path. Tire swings, monkey bars, and a slide were there. It was all heavily vandalized, but still standing. A large building stood behind it, the remains of an old parking lot between them.

As the Covered Man shifted his concentration from the playground to the road in front of him, he heard a cough, as if someone were trying to get his attention.

Shifting his gaze back to the playground, he found a hooded figure perched atop of the monkey bars. For an instant, he thought he saw four red eyes in the shape of a cross underneath the hood, then they were gone. Did he see them? Or was it some kind of imprint in his mind from the thing in the woods?

"Helluva night to be sightseeing." It sounded like an elderly man with a dialect he couldn't place. The Covered Man noticed the old man's robes were free of snow. His hand went to the pistol on his belt.

"Now, now," The figure said, sounding like one would scold a child. "None of that. I mean you no harm. Just wondering about a lone figure out on a night like this." A robed arm gestured skyward toward the bad weather.

"Could ask the same thing."

The robed figure laughed and raised his hands towards its face. The Covered Man instantly drew his pistol. Seeing the weapon, the robed figure slowed his movements. He drew back the hood, revealing a man in his late fifties or early sixties. His hair was white as the snow, his face clean shaven.

"Name's Voclin." With a cunning smile, as if he already knew the answer, he asked, "Care to show me your face, stranger? Or tell me your name?"

"No." The Covered Man replaced the pistol in its holster.

"Again, I ask, what brings you out on a night like this?"

"Passing through."

"Few visitors these days. Dangerous area since it's so close to MadTown. Pair that up with our babbler problem, no wonder few come here. Used to be only a few of those babbler things here and there, but since someone shooed them out of the settlement to the west, they seem to have taken up residence here. Luckily, those decadent humans don't like the cold. One of the few safe times to be out these days."

"In a hurry."

"Why didn't you say so? Need a vehicle? I think I have an old truck I could spare you."

The Covered Man nodded in acceptance. He disliked trusting most people, but with the black car gone, he needed a way to hurry back to Blac Arth as soon as possible to warn of Fappa Jack's return, and pact with the mutants.

The old man beckoned for the Covered Man to follow him into the parking lot. Many types of vehicles were there, most in a state of disrepair. Some of them were stripped down to their frame. Next to the brick building, there was a large blue tarp held up by poles. The edges were held down by brick to make sure it wouldn't blow away in the wind. The snow had been recently removed, as if the old man knew he would need whatever underneath.

"Go ahead," He said, nodding at the makeshift structure.

The Covered Man stepped up to it and pulled the tarp back. It flapped in the wind as he did. A four-by-four truck resided beneath. It had very little rust on it. If he didn't know when and where he was, we could swear the truck could have been on any used car lot in the BeforeTimes.

"Get in. I need a lift to Highway 14. If you do that favor for me, it's yours."

The Covered Man still suspected a trap. Yet he didn't sense any foreboding or misgivings from the stranger. He went around the driver's side and got in. The old man climbed in the passenger's side.

"Check the visor."

The Covered Man flipped down the visor and the keys fell into his lap.

"Uses BeforeTime ignition?"

"Call me a sucker for those times."

"Hhhh." He put the key in the ignition and it roared into life.

The engine purred as the truck slowly moved from its plastic cocoon. Everything worked in the vehicle. The lights. The windshield wipers. Even the heater. It had been years since he had even seen a vehicle in this good of condition, much less drive one.

Pulling out of the parking lot onto the street, he headed southward to 'the 14', but curiosity got the better of him.

"Been through here a few times for supplies. Never seen before."

The old man chuckled, "I've been around."

The Covered Man slowed down to avoid a burnt out derelict vehicle he knew he was approaching even before he saw it. He knew it was there since he was the one who destroyed it.

"How about you son? What are you doing out in this storm?"

"No one's son."

"Surely you have family?"

"Helluva night for you to walk back."

The old man just smiled at him. A knowing smile a father would give to their child the first time they rode their bike successfully without falling.

"The People will speak only of greed. Horrible thoughts will be freely accepted. Many die. Intellectuals will argue fiercely among themselves. Humility will be eradicated." He looked at the Covered Man and punctuated his next sentence, "Then the war began."

The Covered Man almost crashed the vehicle he drove. "Who are you?"

"A man of mystery who met another in the midst of a snowstorm it seems."

The Covered Man drove in silence for a moment. Wondering if he should go for his pistol. "Just what do you remember?"

"Hold your tongue. Your answers are your own."

"But…"

"Turn off the headlights."

"Hhhh?"

"Trust me."

The headlights went off and the darkness of the storm encroached back in upon them. The Covered Man slowed the truck down to make sure he didn't speed off the side of the road.

Below him, at the bottom of a small hill, lay the 14. As he crept along, he saw numerous headlights through the storm. all pointing west. At least twenty vehicles went by before he lost count.

"Are they?"

"Going to Blac Arth? Yes. Jack is going to wipe the settlement from existence. The choice is now yours. Will you be the destructor, or the savior?"

The Covered Man turned to his passenger, determined to stop this dance and ask bluntly what he knows of his past.

The passenger seat was empty.

He heard no opening of the door. Reaching over to feel the seat, it wasn't warm. There was no melted snow on it either.

Did he imagine the man in robes? Like the red-eyed thing? This time there was no giant worm about placing things in his thoughts that he knew of. Was he finally losing his mind?

He shook his head. He could worry about his sanity later. Right then, he had to get to Blac Arth while it still stood.

He flicked the lights back on and the tires spit snow behind the truck before they gripped the road. He had to catch up with the attacking vehicles before they reached Blac Arth. Hopefully he could destroy a few and turn the focus of all of them to him, and then he could lure them all away.

The storm still raged, limiting his visibility. More than once, he almost skidded off the road. Cursing the storm, he tried to find a balance between speed and control.

Minutes went by. Still no sign of the horde of steel anywhere ahead of him. The Covered Man cursed himself. Why did he go to scout? He should have stayed with the settlement. If they sent anyone else, though, they would have been dead.

Flashes of the past year reflected in the pool of his mind. The fellow stoicism of Joshua. The sternness of Sike. The optimism of Javier. The kindness of Linda. Rays. If he considered anyone a friend since No Face, it would be him. And Kristine.

He shook his head and subconsciously sped up. They had to be getting close to Blac Arth and still no sign of those he pursued. These settlers looked to him for protection. They had no clue everything was his fault and why he did it. His foot moved to the floor further and further.

The red lights of the mutant's taillight emerged from between the flakes of heavy snow. The Covered Man pulled the steering wheel to the left, attempting to avoid colliding with the other vehicles, to no avail.

There was a collision of tearing metal and breaking glass. The Covered Man felt the steering wheel press against his chest while his head struck the dashboard. He landed in the middle of an angry beehive someone just kicked.

Flames leaped from the front of his truck. He slammed into the back of a car with spikes all over it, now over on its side. Next to it, another car sat, the entire driver's side caved in.

A mutant with a chameleon shaped head threw open the door, cold clawed hands wrapped around his leg and pulled him from the vehicle.

He drew the knife from his belt and drove it into the mutant's stomach, freeing his left arm he pushed it off the road and into the ditch.

They were on the western side of the bridge over the creek. Recalling how the original settlers helped get his black car over the creek when he first arrived fueled his rage. They fixed that bridge so they could scout more. Encourage trade. But it was a two-way street. Now the mutants used it to launch their attack.

There were four vehicles at the rear guard on the bridge. Ahead, he saw some kind of large vehicle, like a fire truck fitted with a catapult. It was lit up by the fiery wreckage it launched over the wall into the settlement.

The projectiles lit the area up like a shooting star every time they were launched, until they struck the wall. They burned out in explosions of flame, sending burning fragments in all directions. Then, the wall was enveloped by the storm as the flames diminished, until the next projectile hurtled forth.

He didn't have time to watch the fireworks. Three new mutants ran toward him: A jackal with a rusty tire iron, a tiger with one eye in the middle of its forehead wielding a hatchet, and a wolf that held a knife in each hand with three more in a bandolier across its chest.

The jackal swung the tire iron directly at his head, but the Covered Man parried it with the knife, giving it a solid knee to its stomach and leaving it doubled over and coughing.

The wolf and the tiger maneuvered to approach from opposite sides. Feigning at the wolf, he pivoted and sliced at the tiger's wrist that held the hatchet. Before it finished tumbling to the snow-covered road, a well-placed kick sent it over the side of the bridge, about five feet into the freezing water below.

The wolf's lips curled into a snarl. It reached back and hurtled a knife with all its might, but the Covered Man read its movements. With the bad weather obscuring the wolf's vision, he easily blocked the incoming projectile with his own blade.

Pulling another knife from its bandolier, it lunged at him. Anticipating the creature's attack, the Covered Man's knife deflected the blade, steering the mutant away from him. The momentum carried the wolf past the Covered Man.

As the mutant tried to slow itself and turn to face its prey, it slipped on the snow. Instinct kicked in and it threw its arms out wide to regain balance. It regained its footing, but its reward for staying upright was a knife thrust into the back of its neck, killing it instantly.

Taking a rag from his pocket, the Covered Man wiped off the blade, then returned both.

As he walked past the jackal mutant struggling to regain its feet, it snarled at him, "Human meat. Food for the collective."

The Covered Man lashed out with a foot, kicking it in the side of the head and sending it to the ground, unmoving. He moved past its broken form, toward the vehicle raining fire down the burning buildings of Blac Arth.

The glow from many burning buildings pierced the snowy, nighttime sky. He could see the silhouettes of dozens of misshapen mutants running through the storm.

On the truck launching wreckage over the wall stood a form that could have been the Covered Man's twin. Its shouts were half words and half grunts, bellowing calls for the humans to surrender.

At the rear of the same truck were two mutants, a lion humanoid with a lobster claw for an arm, and a bear with red fur were loading a ruined engine into the catapult. Also standing next to the launching device, operating what must be the aiming mechanism, stood a human.

To be heard over the gunfire and explosions, the human shouted, "Hurry up, you scrubs! We need to get this wall down!" The voice pegged the human as Fappa Jack.

The two mutants shoved the engine fully onto the arm of the catapult and the bear grunted, "Go." The two mutants turned and wandered off to get the next projectile to launch.

"Pull that lever, and you'll be dead before it lands," the Covered Man said.

"Owl? Is that you? Wondered why you didn't jump out to save these fools when we launched the attack this time around."

"Foolish as serving those who will eat you?"

"Cut the high and mighty crap. You know those norms don't care about you. They never told you about me, did they?"

"Nothing to tell."

"Oh really? For almost a year before you wandered out of the wastelands, me and my gang protected these ungrateful wretches from the mutants of Madtown. We took tribute and paid most of it to the mutants. Even you must have seen how these things are spreading out over the area like locusts. They will rule this area and everything around MadTown for a hundred kilometers by this time next year."

The Covered Man listened, but kept scanning the area in cast the mutants returned.

"But then you came along. Killing off Bum Bag. Killing most of my gang. Those of us who survived *had* to go to the Big Beast and beg for help. With any luck, he will only kill most of my ex-followers instead of all of them, and things can go back to the way they were."

The Covered Man just stared at Jack.

"Yeah. That's right, Owl." Fappa waved a hand toward the burning wall and the sounds of screams and gunshots. "This is all your fault! If you just traded and went on your way, these dirt scratchers would have lived out their difficult lives, but at least they would have lived."

The lion and the bear emerged from the darkness, the former dragging an old statue of George Washington while the latter carried what looked like a gas drum.

Fappa continued. "Understand. All this is your fault! You destroyed everything with your actions."

The Covered Man staggered back, the sound of billions screaming echoed in his mind. Snapping back to the present, Fappa Jack had his back to him, fleeing in between the vehicles.

Before he could give chase, a two-foot lobster claw arched through the air toward his head. He raised his right arm and the claw snapped tight around it. Pain shot through his body, but at least it didn't grip him by the head.

The red bear used this to its advantage and tore at him with its claws. Grabbing the pistol, he unloaded a full clip into the bear's open mouth. The pellets of metal ripped through the back of its skull, and it crumpled to the ground.

Using the clawed lion's leverage against him, he propelled himself toward it so he could grasp it around the neck. Its eyes went wide with fear as it tried to increase pressure on the Covered Man's arm.

"Stronger than you," he said. A soft crunch came from the lion's neck as both its larynx and spinal cord collapsed.

He only had moments before something happened upon the bodies. Pulling the pin on one of his grenades, he moved the gas drum next to the back of the truck and rolled the grenade to its base, then moved around to behind some kind of vehicle used for transporting supplies.

The resounding explosion engulfed the gas drum, and after a split second, the truck it stood by. He felt the heat of the blast from behind the transport.

Flaming debris once again fell from the sky, this time on the outer side of the wall. About three dozen burning mutants clutched at their fur and scales, trying to put themselves out. Some fell and rolled around in the snow. Only a few of them tried to stand back up. The smell of roasting flesh permeated the air.

No sign of Jack, though. Did he run through the gap in the wall? Or off into the dark? The Covered Man strode forward, putting a new clip into his pistol. A mutant with a bat's head and wings came screeching at him from out of the dark, one of its leathery wings still burning. Two well-placed shots to the head dropped it into the snow.

He walked to the destroyed section of wall. Dead and wounded lay everywhere. Multiple buildings were ablaze. Near the opening, lying on his back, was Dor. A spear was driven through his chest, and some kind of claw or bite mark had torn open his eye and half of his face. His remaining eye stared blankly up into the snowy skies.

"Hey!" Rays shouted from atop the northern section of the broken wall. In between the falling snow and the billowing smoke, he could see a trickle of blood from a gash on his right temple.

"Should have guessed that explosion was you."

Linda appeared next to him and Kristine directly behind her. Both held rifles.

The Covered Man climbed a pile of nearby wreckage to get onto the wall where they stood, "Blac Arth okay?"

Rays lacked his normal optimism and just stood in silence.

Joshua shouted at the man in black, "What took you so long? You were supposed to warn us! Everything we tried so hard to build lies in ruins! Almost everyone is dead." After a few seconds he added, "Blac Arth is dead."

A figure leaped onto the wall behind Joshua. Brutish and covered in charred tiger-striped fur, it wore a black loincloth and a black executioner hood over its head. This must be the Big Beast.

Joshua only had enough time to turn around before the thing raked its claws across his throat, sending him spiraling to the ground, leaving a trail of crimson. As he struck the ground, a pool of red spread across the snow beneath him. Both his life and the dreams of the settlement he built drained away.

Big Beast turned toward Rays and his family. Rays shot it in the chest with his rifle, but it seemed to only make Big Beast angrier.

"Only when humans are gone can the new age begin." It crouched and took a stance like a cat about to play with a mouse before it tore it apart.

Linda threw her arms around Rays, half to protect and half out of her feelings. Rays held his arms out wide to protect his family.

Big Beast stepped forward with his arm raised, ready to disembowel its targets.

One arm grasped the mutant around the neck, the other grabbed its upraised arm to try and stop its descent. The Covered Man only managed to slow it. It struck Rays across the chest, directly under where Linda held him, knocking them both off the battlements to the ground below. Big Beast tore at the Covered Man.

"Told...about...you." It coughed as its attacker tried to crush its windpipe."Jack? Beat his last champion. Beat you."

The mutant spun and jumped, anything to shake the Covered Man from its back. It still choked out an inhuman laugh. "Not his champion, human. My pet. Another lapdog. Realizing his superiors." Its speech became slower as the Covered Man's powerful grip took its toll.

The mutant looked at Kristine, who had been slowly backing away from them. It lunged at her with its one free claw, outstretched to rend her open, intent on tearing her intestines from her body.

The Covered Man released his grip on Big Beast's neck to grab the mutant's outstretched arm. He slammed his knee into its back before his feet touched the wall's battlement.

Losing interest in Kristine, Big Beast spun around, breaking the Covered Man's grip on its arms, and able to face its attacker.

"You're the human my pet was so afraid of? Humans are afraid of such petty things."

The Covered Man squared off against his opponent, both searching for weaknesses in the other's defenses.

"I personally led the brigade to hunt and devour the humans of MadTown. Helping the Mind to make it the mutant stronghold it is today. What have you done? Gave these pathetic clumps of meat a sliver of hope. A sliver I have taken away!"

Instinct took over and Big Beast raised its head and roared. It roared to the sky and the storm. It roared for the hundreds of humans it feasted on over the years. It roared as it gave into the bestial blood rage all mutants possess.

The Covered Man connected one of his huge black boots with Big Beast's groin, causing it to choke off its roar and double over. "Mutants weak because slaves to instinct. Humans superior." He landed a solid punch to the hooded face.

His words struck it harder than the punch. It fought through its pain and reared up to block the Covered Man's next blow with its forearm.

The Covered Man found himself on the defense as blow upon blow descended upon him. With its sloppy fighting prowess, he blocked all the attacks, but still had to back up to the break in the wall from the ferocity of the strikes.

One of the mutant's strikes almost knocked him from the wall. As he tried to regain his balance, Big Beast sunk his claws into his chest.

"Now who is superior, human? Only I will walk away, where your corpse will be feasted upon for days!"

The Big Beast raised its fist, lifting the Covered Man into air while driving the claw deep enough he felt it scrape against his ribcage and pierce his left lung. He reached for his pistol, but Big Beast slapped it out of his hand, sending it spinning off into the darkness on the outer side of the wall.

"Victory, you pathetic, hairless thing. You think your suit can protect you from a mutant's vengeance?"

"Good idea." He reached up and removed the hood from the Big Beast, revealing a hairless, human, baby-like face.

Big Beast tossed the Covered Man from the wall to the ground inside the settlement. He landed on his back. Snowflakes struck his goggles. Big Beast raised its hands to shield its face.

"Human?"

Despite its human-like appearance, its mouth moved in an alien way, "No! Humans are the past!"

Big Beast pounced from the catwalk of the wall upon the Covered Man, claws tearing and shredding whatever it could sink its claws into. He tried again to block the incoming fury of blows, but the deep wound in his chest caused him to wheeze heavily and slow his actions.

He slowly gave ground, across the courtyard where the animal pen was, the residents now all torn to shreds by their attackers.

The Covered Man tried to form an offense. Cutting off Big Beast's air supply worked before. He let the mutant land a glancing blow across his left forearm, then a swift right hook landed square in the thing's throat. It instinctively stretched out its left arm for defense as it tried to recover.

As it staggered back, the Covered Man saw the opportunity to drop his guard enough to draw his blade. He managed a few swift cuts across its chest with an additional strike across its outstretched arm before he saw the opening needed to sink the knife into the creature's misshapen, mucus-coated head.

Big Beast tried to resume its attack, lashing out at the Covered Man's leg, sinking its claws deep. But it was too late. The Covered Man struck with all his might at Big Beast's head.

The blade deflected the mutant's head as if it struck stone. A helping of the mucus stuck to it.

As he pulled the blade back, the metal corroded, a reek of acid pierced the air, and he had to drop it into the snow as it dissolved almost completely away.

The misshaped head grinned at him. "Humans are yesterday. Mutants are the future!"

A lump of black, misshapen flesh wriggled from its mouth and opened up to cough up a glob of acidic spittle, striking him square in the chest. The open wound burned with such pain, the Covered

Man screamed. The spittle consumed the black suit he wore, and it did not grow back.

The two Goliaths faced each other. One without the hood that protected the world from its corrosive bile, the other just having remnants of the suit that protected him over his head, hands, and legs.

"You fight well, human. But you are just delaying the inevitable. We *are* the future."

"The future is talking me to death."

With a wicked smile, the Big Beast charged. Again, its claws descended on his human opponent.

The one from the BeforeTime had a plan, but he was not sure his body would last much longer. His breathing came even heavier as the acidic spittle inflamed the wound in his chest even worse.

He gave ground again, to the house directly across the street from the Box. It was one of the buildings that was burning brightly. It was the house of David, the one whose music convinced him to stay here, despite everything else telling him to move on.

Seemed a fitting place to die.

Big Beast lunged its right claw at his midsection, but he deflected its blow away enough that he could drive his knee into its chin. The Big Beast staggered back from the blow, but the mucus ate away at the black suit where it struck his opponent.

He retrieved a grenade from his belt and prepared to toss it at the mutant, but it recovered faster than he suspected and slapped the hand that held the grenade with such force he let go of the dangerous device, sending it spinning away into the air toward the building. When it detonated, it sent flaming splinters of debris through the air like javelins. The Covered Man felt a two-foot piece lodge into the back of his left shoulder before the force of the blast sent him almost face first into the snow.

A large, clawed hand stopped him from falling. As it forced him to his stay on his feet, he saw Big Beast fared no better. It stood above him with three smaller still burning splinters piercing through its left arm and shoulder and one through its right eye.

"Won't even… feast on your corpse… human. I'll mount your head from the gates of MadTown."

Big Beast clenched its right hand into a fist and slammed it into the Covered Man's head, cracking the left lens of his goggles. He saw the fragments of the lens tumble to the ground in slow motion, like black snowflakes.

With all his might, he grabbed Big Beast's fist as it drew it back for another strike and used all his strength to push against the mutants' elbow, forcing it to bend the wrong way.

It howled in pain and let go of the Covered Man, allowing him to tumble earthward. As he hit the snow, Big Beast used its still operational arm to tear the chunk of wood out of his shoulder. It raised the splinter of wood above its head, a wild look in its eyes of triumph flashed across its face.

The roar of a shotgun tore through the storm, and Big Beast's chest tore open with buckshot. Its eyes went wide as it tumbled to the snowy ground next to the Covered Man.

Behind it was Rays, reloading both barrels of his shotgun. He strode over to where Big Beast lay, raised the shotgun, and said, "Humans aren't as weak as you think." And unloaded both shells directly into the front of its chest, tearing what remained of its internal organs to ribbons.

Rays stared at the remains of Big Beast for a moment to make sure it would not threaten anyone again. When satisfied, he turned to check on the Covered Man. He attempted to push himself to a standing position. His left arm was cradled against his chest, partially to cover the wound in his chest, partially the pain from his shoulder didn't allow him to move it much.

Rays strode over to help the Covered Man to his feet.

"You look terrible."

"Yeah."

"The Box and the Shop are still intact. Let me help you back." As he moved to assist the other man, he looked directly into his eye for the first time and withdrew.

"At least take the shotgun," he said and tossed it to his friend. The Covered Man caught it and looked and the butt of it. It had "Rays and Linda" engraved on it.

Looking back at Rays, the other man just nodded for a moment and then dug in his pocket. "You might be able to scare people away with your appearance, but take these just in case." He flung a small bag of shells at the Covered Man, which he snatched out of the air. Depositing the contents into a belt pouch, the Covered Man turned away from Blac Arth. He was coming for Jack.

EPILOGUE

Fappa Jack fled across the field of new fallen snow.

They will all pay. Every last one of them. He thought as he moved through the endless sea of white.

Pulling his feet up through the snow became tiring, even with his fury to drive him forward. Looking behind him, the burning remains of Blac Arth could not even be seen any more. The distance he put between himself and the accursed place, doing part of the job, but the storm did the majority.

All of them. They will pay. There were many without hope, many without family. He would give them that. He shouldn't have trusted a bunch of mindless mutants to do what needed to be done. He needed to find a way to lead them. To control them.

Reaching the edge of a forest of young saplings, he took advantage of the concealment to stop. Checking to see if he still had his pistol and the numerous knives he kept on him, he felt it okay to rest. He put the palms of his hands on his knees and doubled over, gasping for air.

I'll show the Owl. He will wish he never crawled out of whatever hole he came from. Some day he will scream my name as I peel off that costume he wears, as I will peel the skin from the man underneath.

As he inhaled to ease the pain of exhaustion, he saw feet standing in the snow a few paces away. Without looking up, Jack knew who it was.

"Manny." He said,

"Jack."

Jack stood and raised to his full height and stared at him.

"Get out of my way traitor."

"Come back with me. We can rebuild Blac Arth together."

Jack stepped forward planted a finger on Manny's chest, "Rebuild it? I just destroyed it!"

"You and your new friends didn't damage anything that cannot be rebuilt. Our sense of community."

Jack removed his finger from Manny and looked exasperated, "Oh please! You people are evil. No problems paying tribute to me for months to protect you from the mutants, and the first chance you get you stab me in the back."

"We just wanted to be left alone. Both from the mutants and from you."

Jack's rage burned within him. It was bad enough to lose again to that stranger, but to have Manny offer his false sympathy became too much to bear.

Manny could sense Jack's anger, he knew the other man well. He desperately wanted Jack to come back with him to the settlement, and believed he had a good chance to get him to do so, now that he had nowhere else to go.

He reached out and put his hand on Jack's shoulder. "Please. Just hear me out Jack…"

In an instant, Jack whirled around, knife in hand, and buried it up to the hilt in Manny's neck.

"J-Jack…" Manny said again, as he fell back into the snow, his life staining it crimson as it leaked out.

Jack said nothing as he replaced his blade and renewed his flight into the forest.